TITLE I MATERIALS

Georgetown Elementary School
Indian Prairie School District
Aurora, Illinois

EXPLORER

THE MYSTERY BOXES

SEVEN GRAPHIC STORIES

EDITED BY **KAZU KIBUISHI**

AMULET BOOKS
NEW YORK

THANKS TO MY COEDITOR,
SHEILA KEENAN
—K.K.

Cataloging-in-Publication Data has been applied for
and may be obtained from the Library of Congress.

Paperback ISBN 978-1-4197-0009-5
Hardcover ISBN 978-1-4197-0010-1

Cover art © 2011 Kazu Kibuishi
Book design by Chad W. Beckerman

Text and illustrations © 2012 by the individual artists as follows:
"Under the Floorboards," pages 4–21, © 2012 Emily Carroll
"Spring Cleaning," pages 22–39, text © 2012 Dave Roman
and Raina Telgemeier
"The Keeper's Treasure," pages 40–57, © 2012 Jason Caffoe
"The Butter Thief," pages 58–75, © 2012 Rad Sechrist
"The Soldier's Daughter," pages 76–93, © 2012 Stuart Livingston
"Whatzit," pages 94–109, © 2012 Johane Matte
"The Escape Option," pages 110–127, © 2012 Kazu Kibuishi

Printed and bound in China
10 9 8 7 6 5 4 3 2

Amulet Books are available at special discounts when purchased in quantity
for premiums and promotions as well as fundraising or educational use.
For details, contact specialsales@abramsbooks.com, or the address below.

ABRAMS
THE ART OF BOOKS SINCE 1949
115 West 18th Street
New York, NY 10011
www.abramsbooks.com

CONTENTS

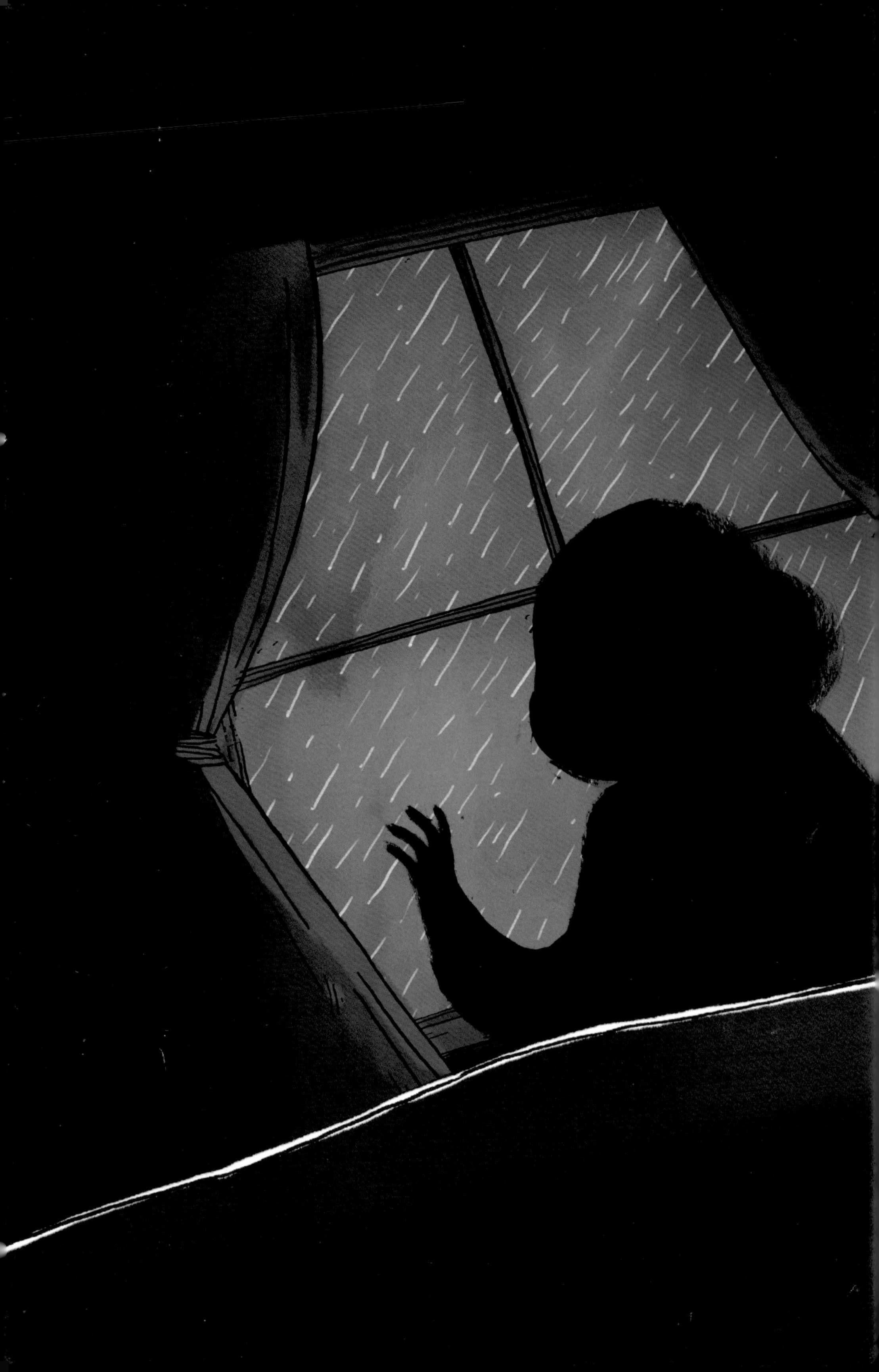

UNDER the FLOORBOARDS

BY EMILY CARROLL

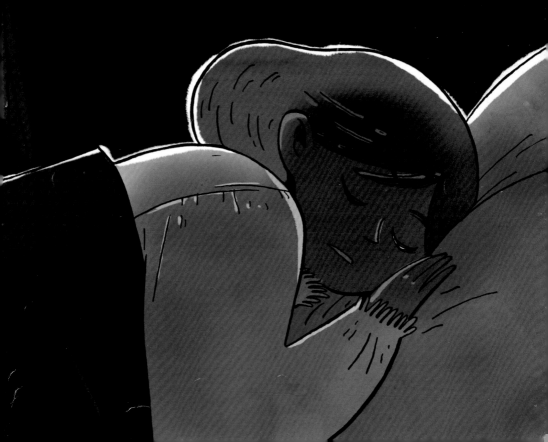

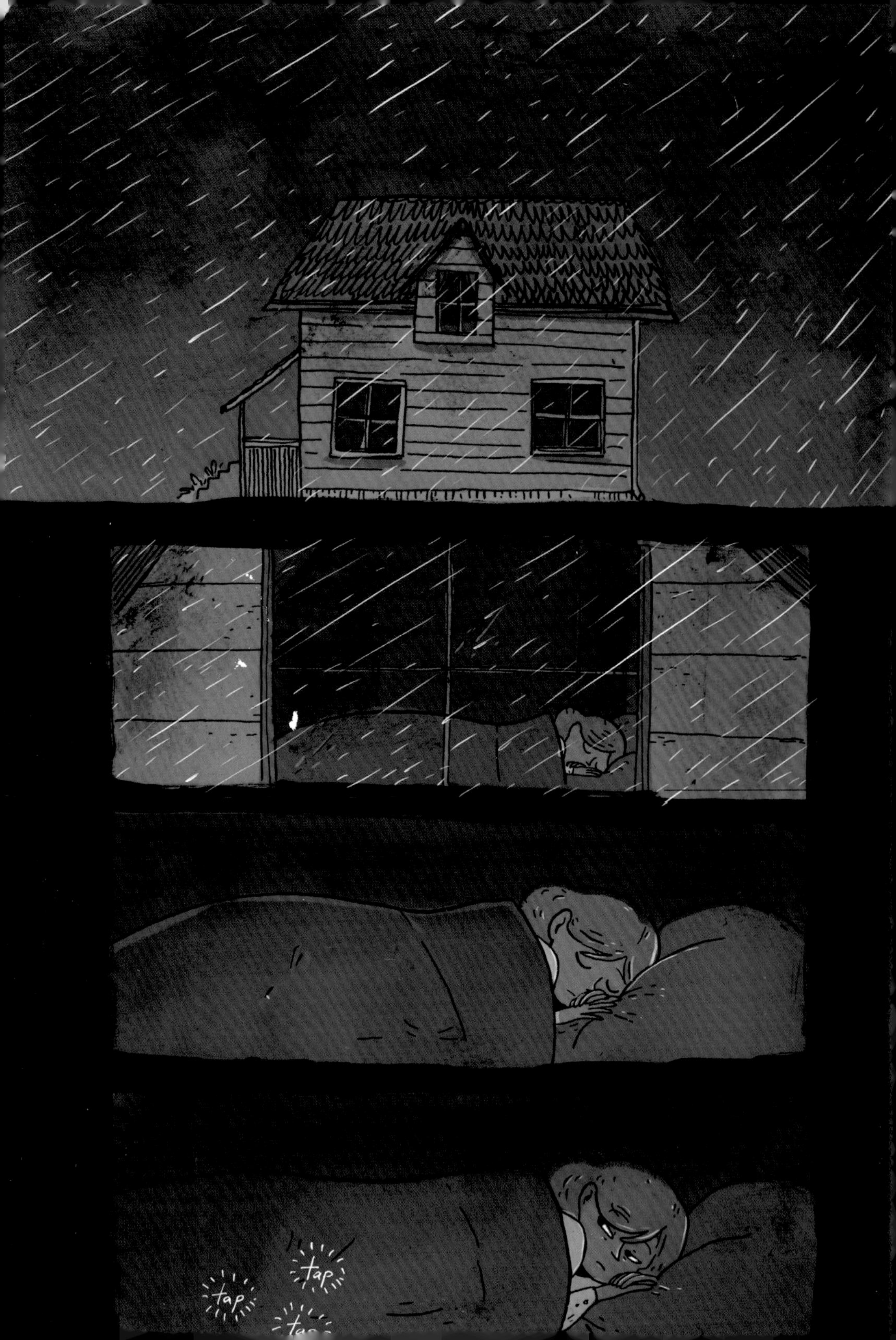
tap
tap

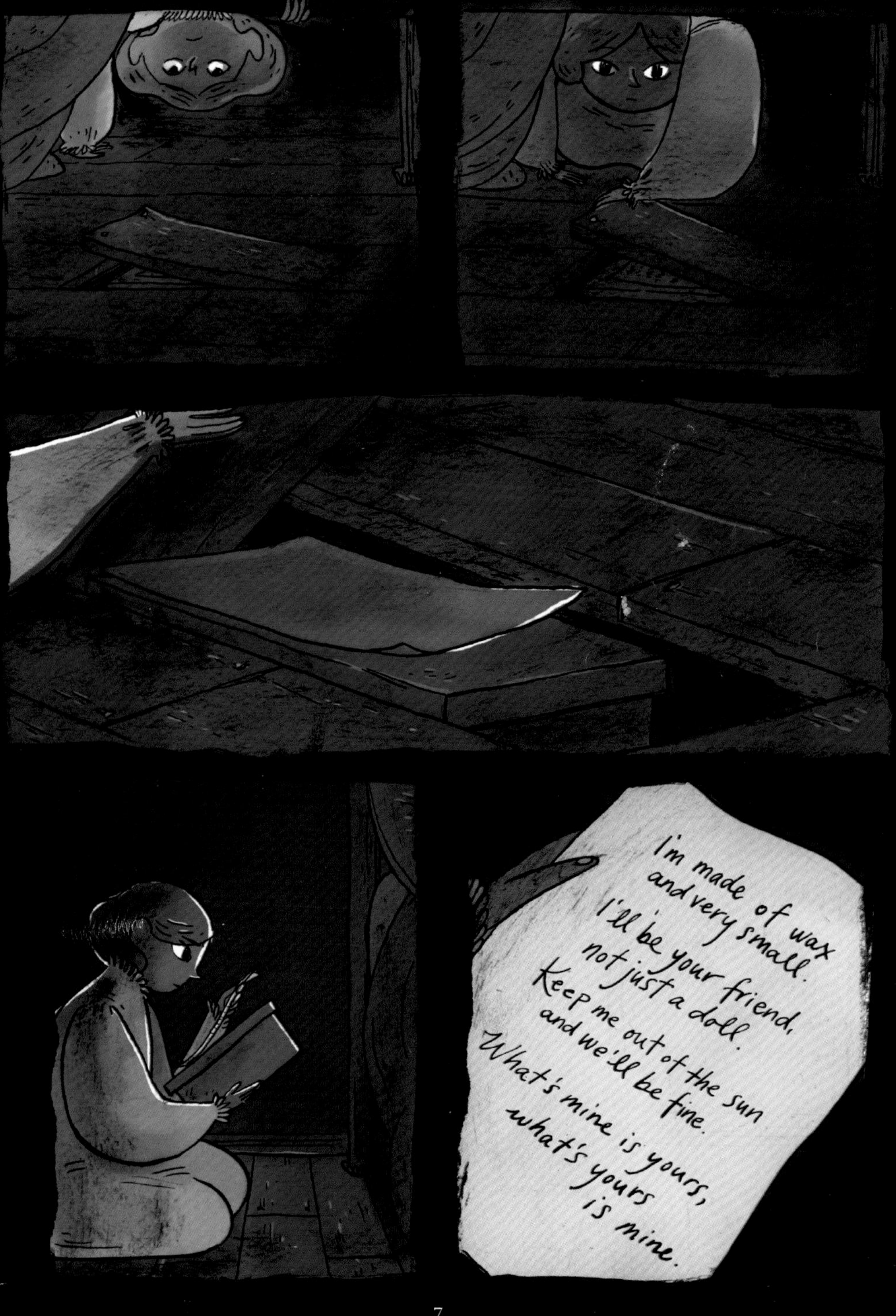
I'm made of wax
and very small.
I'll be your friend,
not just a doll.
Keep me out of the sun
and we'll be fine.
What's mine is yours,
what's yours
is mine.

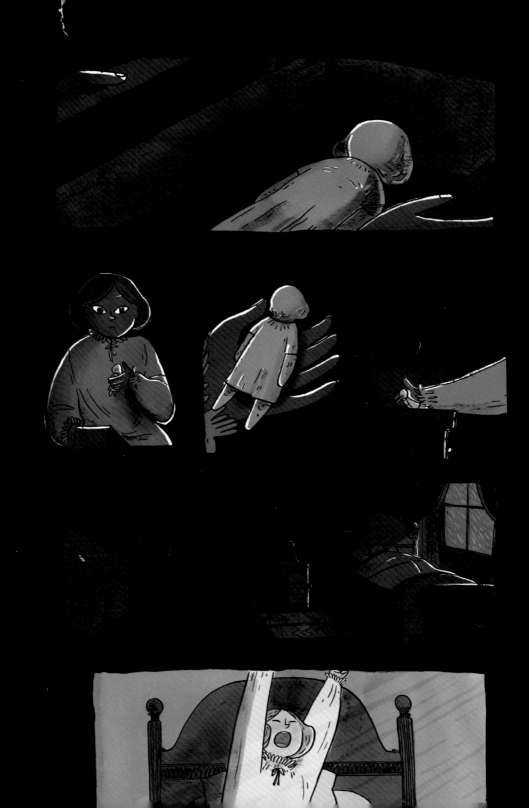

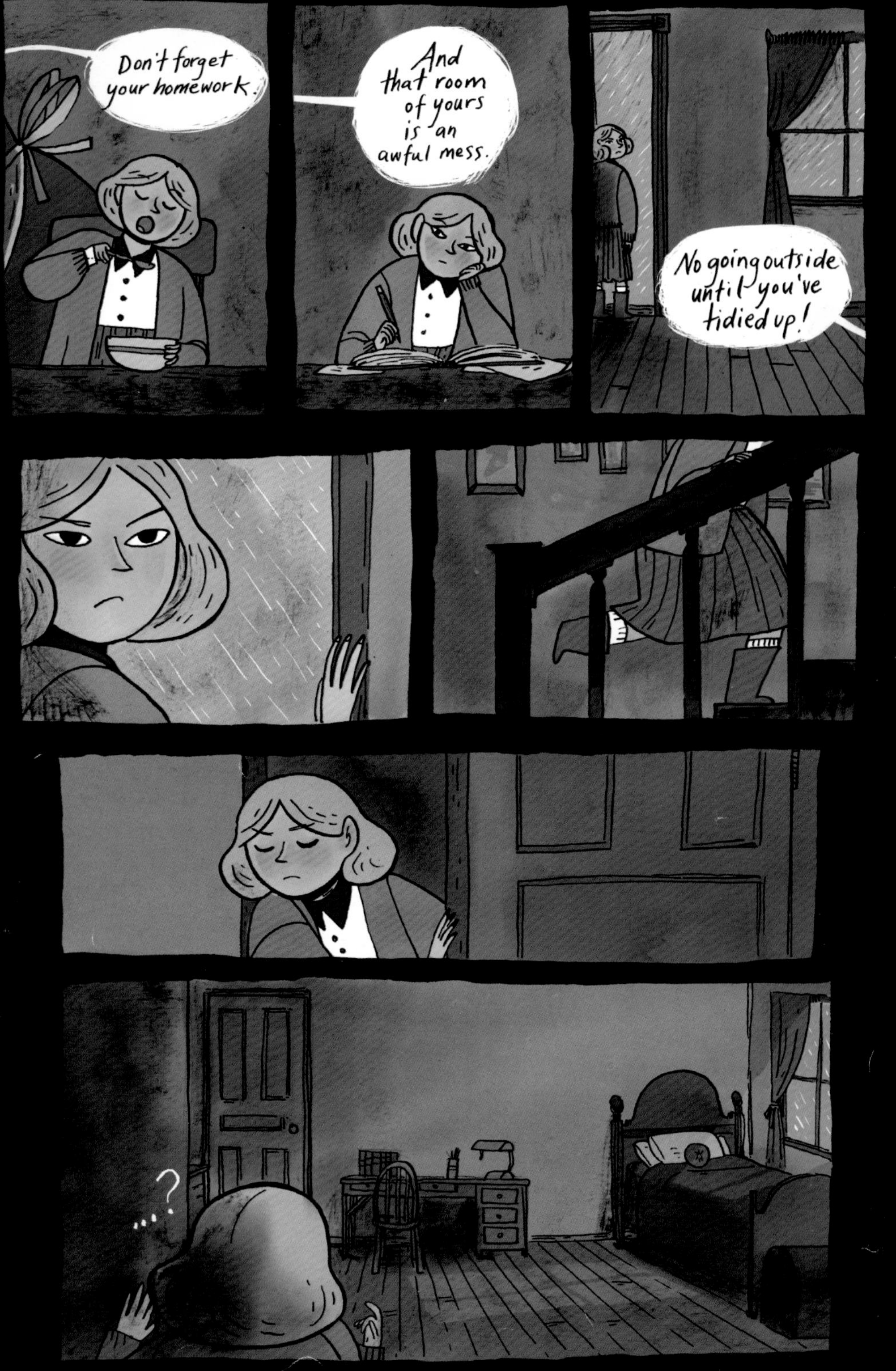
Don't forget your homework.
And that room of yours is an awful mess.
No going outside until you've tidied up!
...?

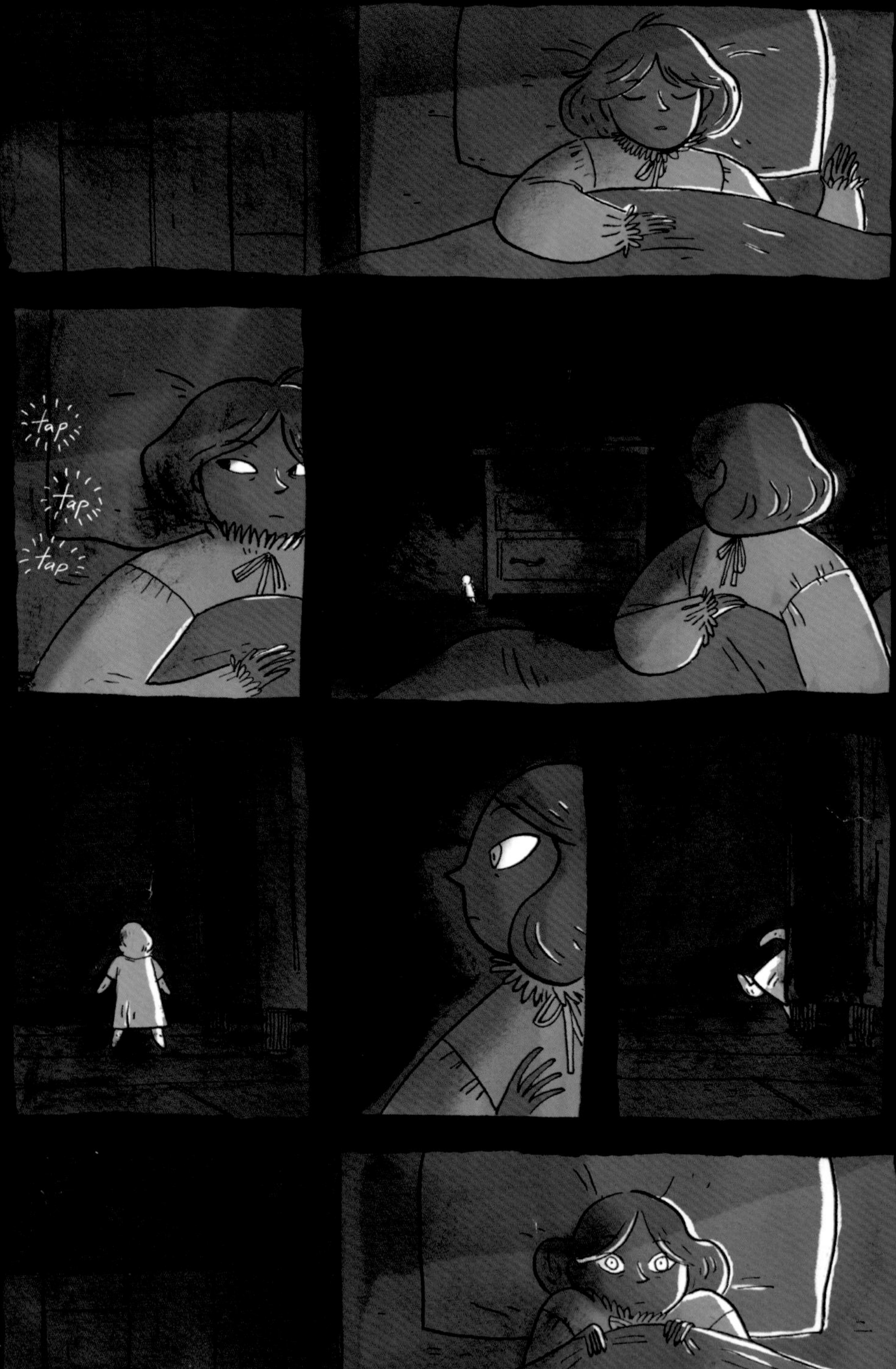
tap
tap
tap

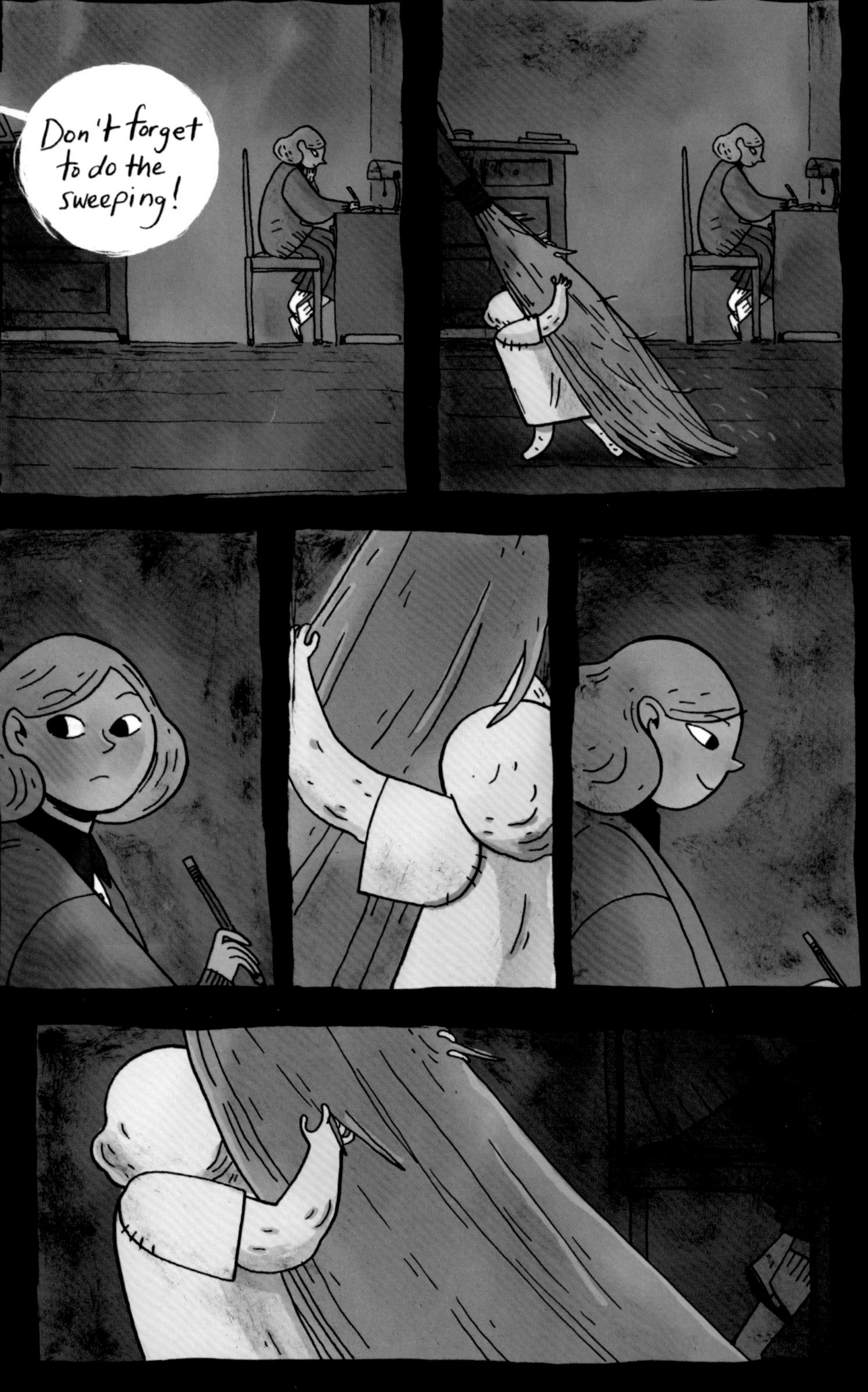
Don't forget to do the sweeping!

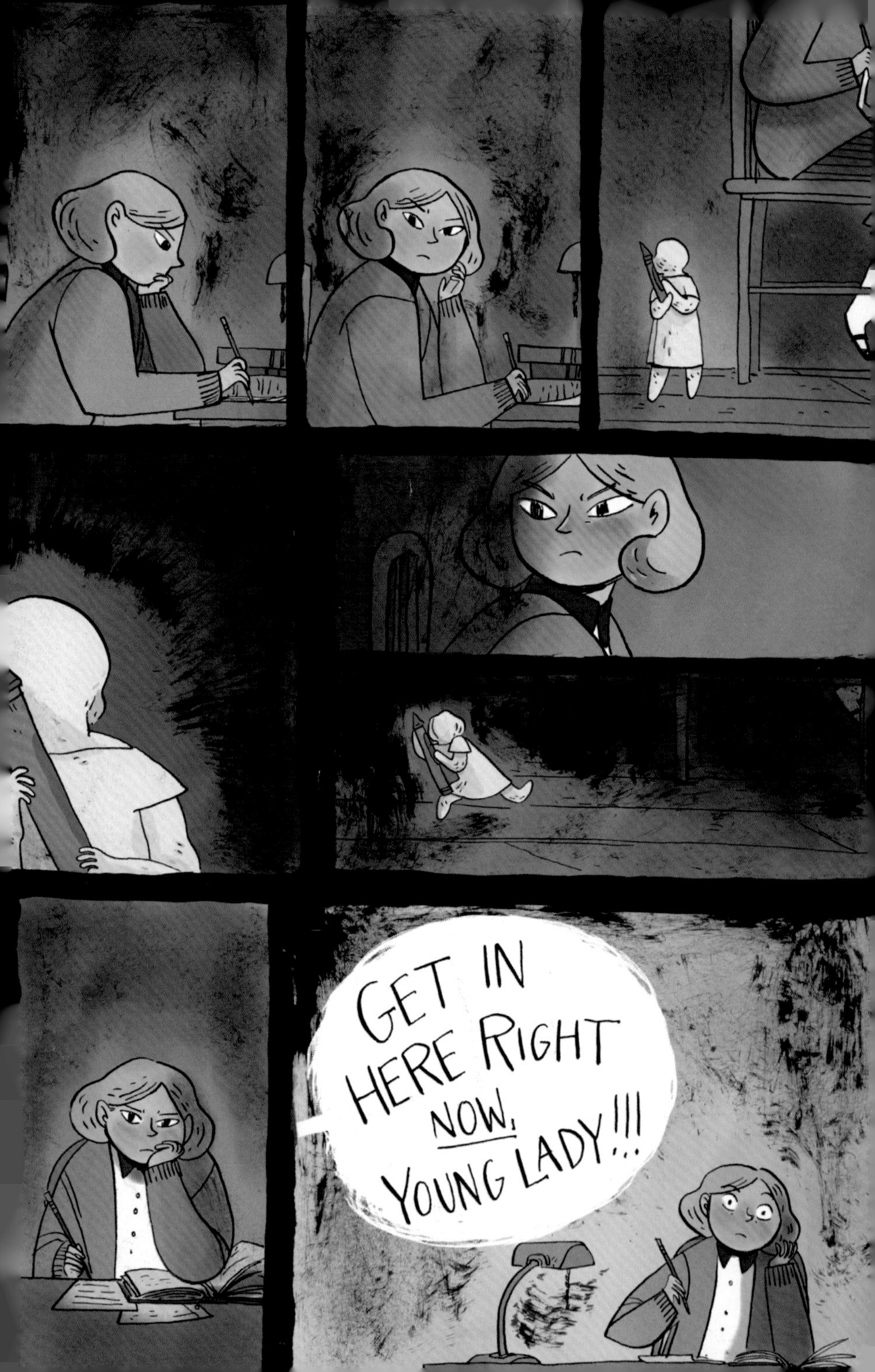
GET IN HERE RIGHT NOW, YOUNG LADY!!!

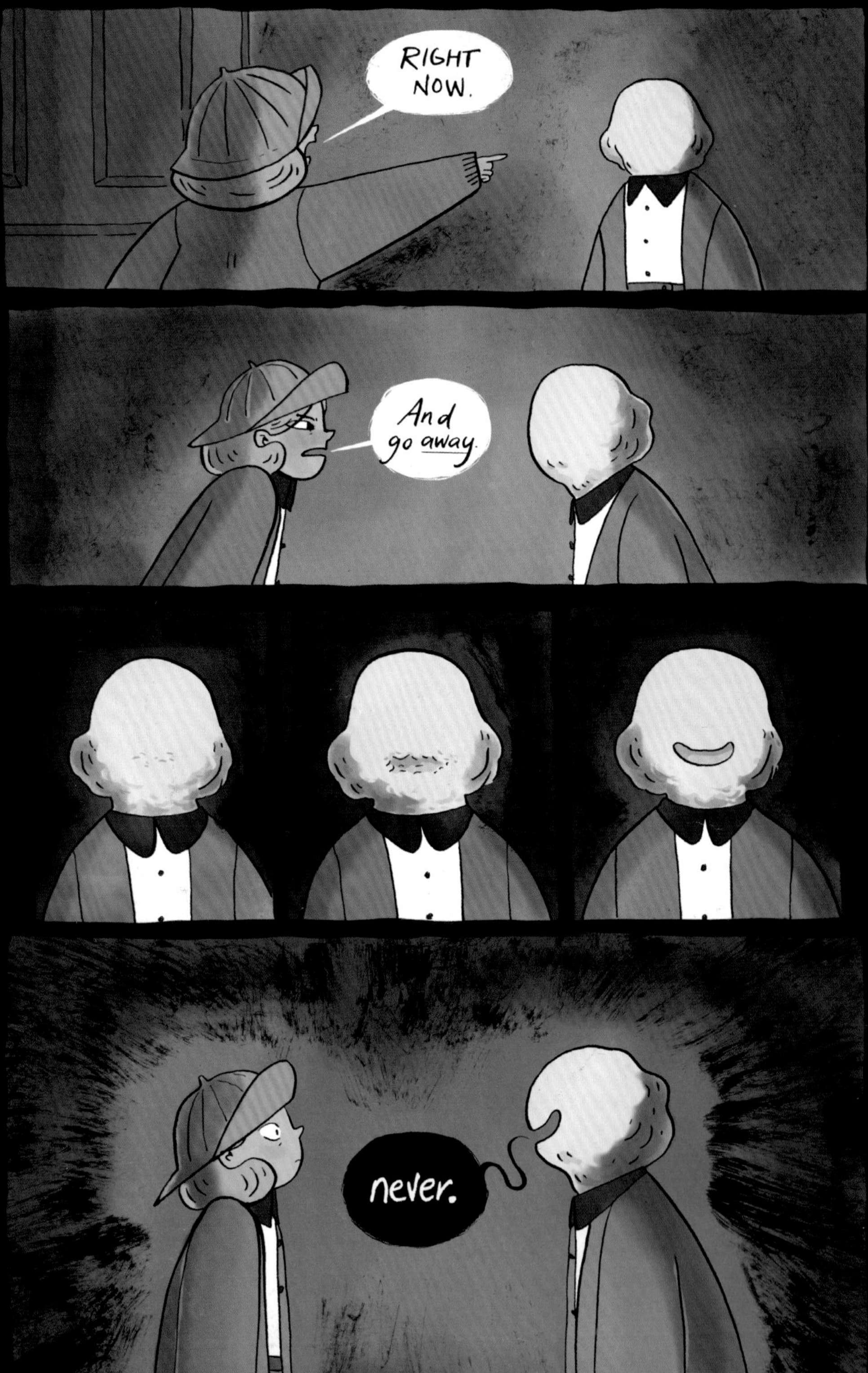
RIGHT NOW.
And go away.
never.

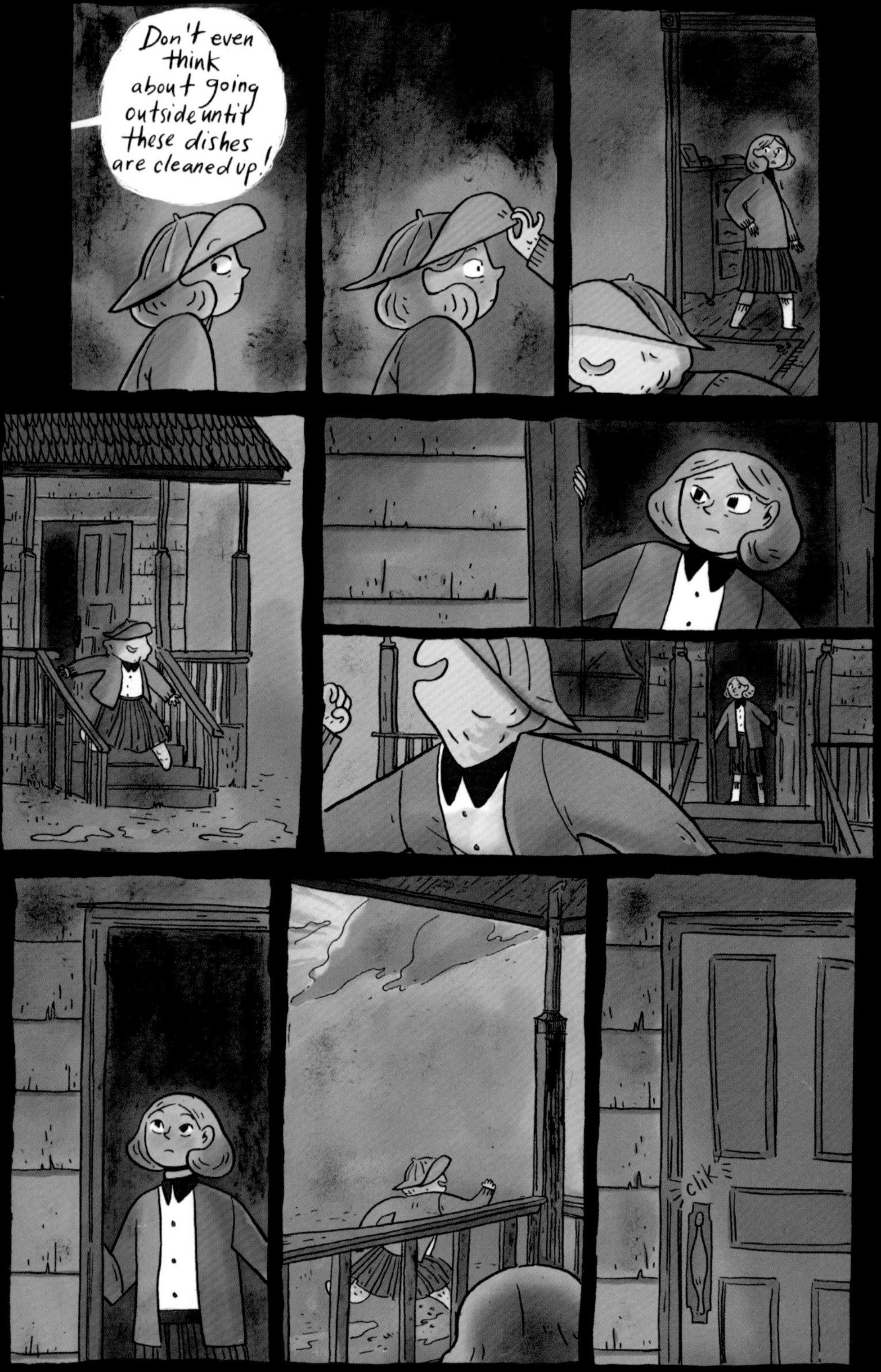
Don't even think about going outside until these dishes are cleaned up!
CLIK

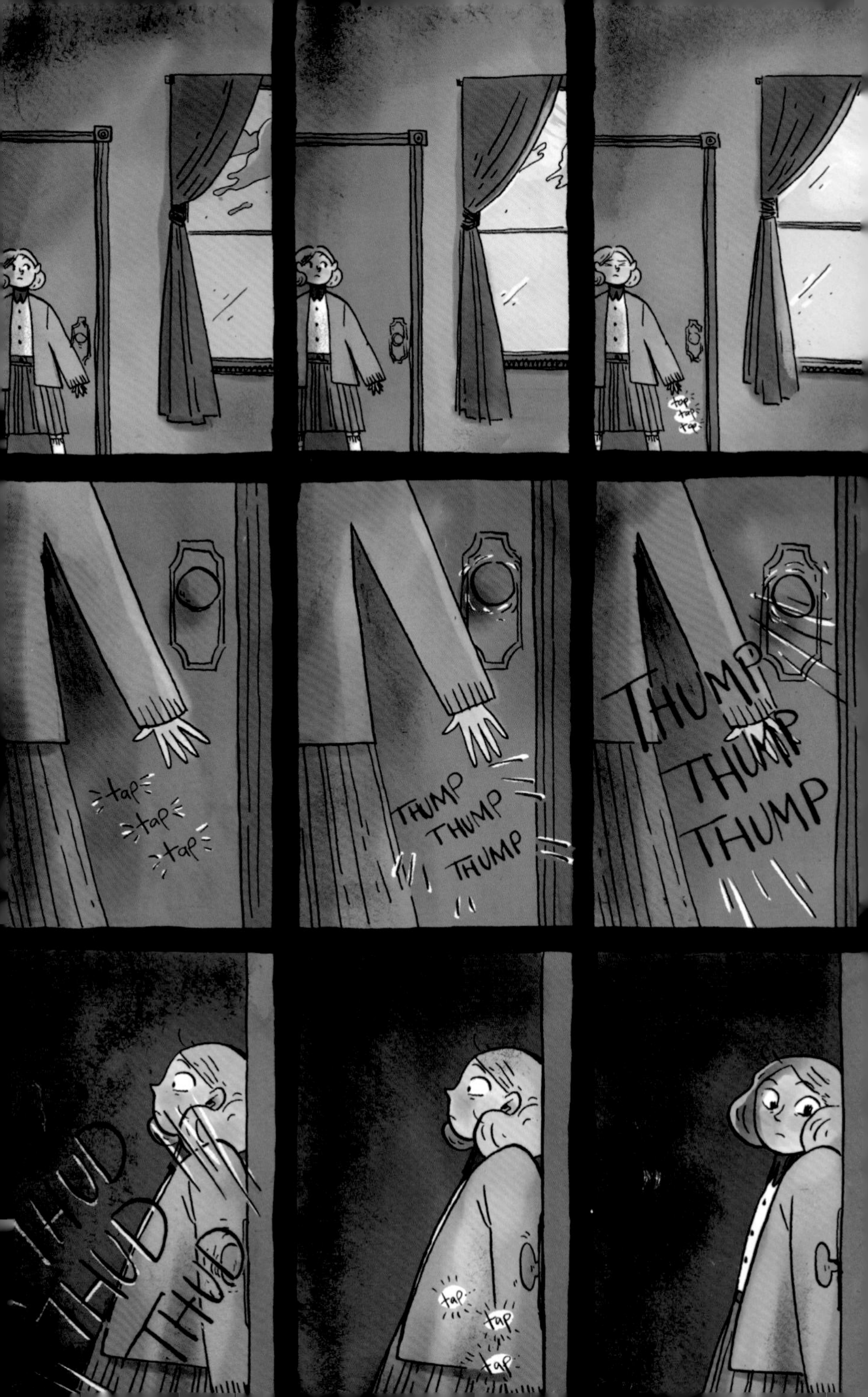
tap
tap
tap
tap
tap
tap
THUMP
THUMP
THUMP
THUMP
THUMP
THUMP
THUD
THUD
THUD
tap
tap
tap

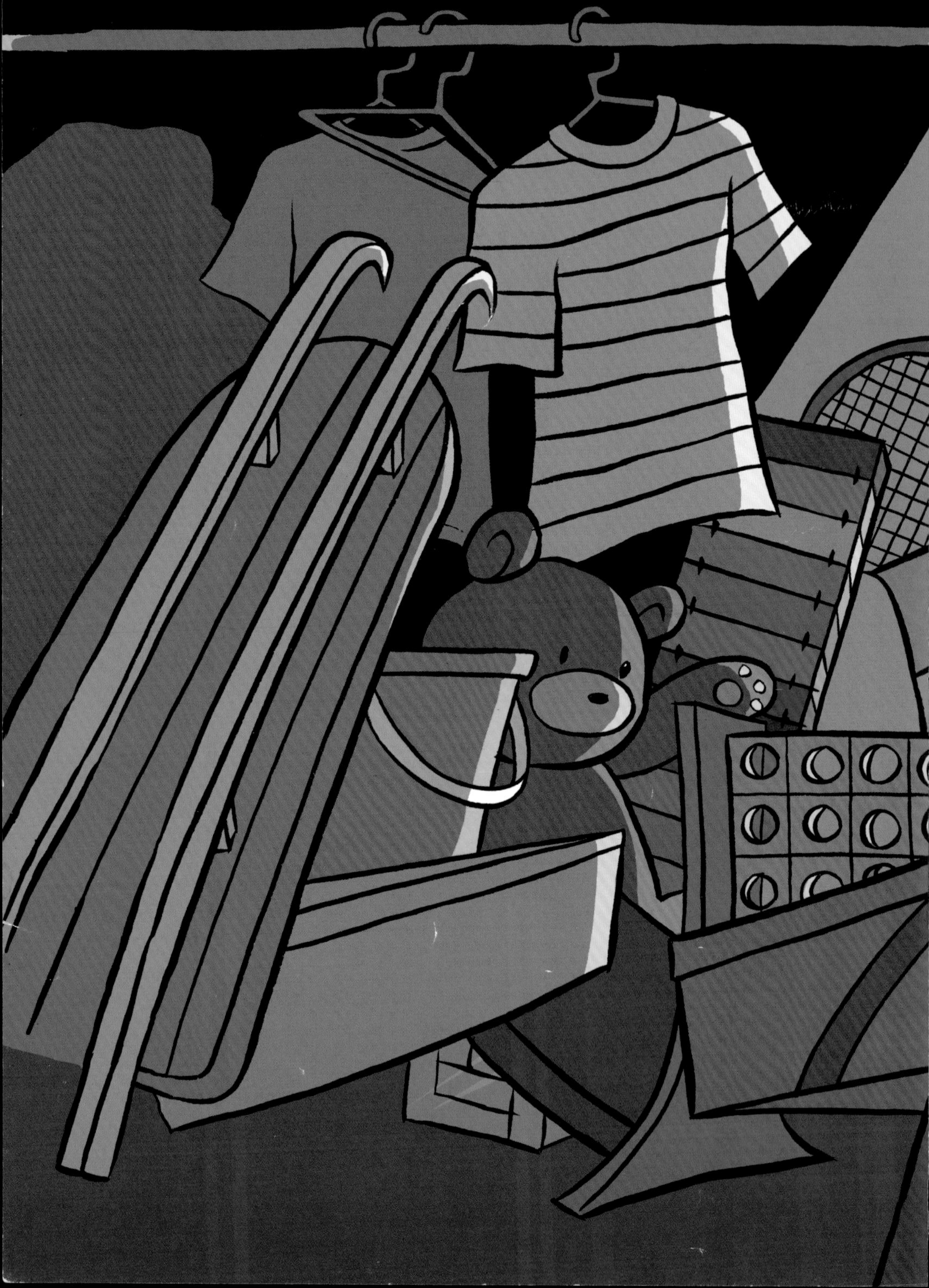

Spring Cleaning

BY DAVE ROMAN
& RAINA TELGEMEIER

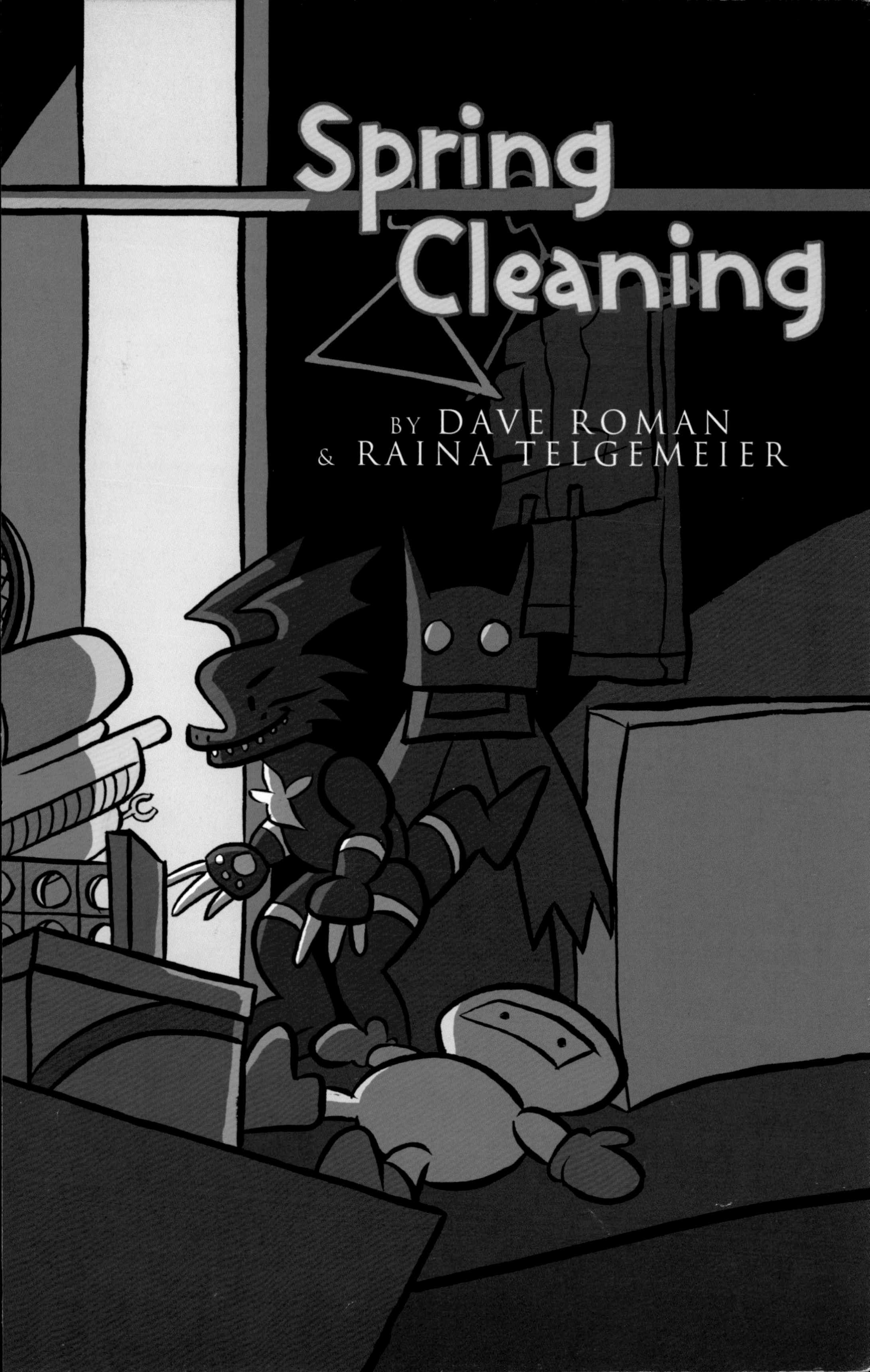

Y'KNOW, BRO, YOU COULD SELL SOME OF THIS STUFF ON eBUY!

I BET YOU COULD MAKE ENOUGH MONEY TO AFFORD SOME NEW VIDEO GAMES! LIKE SKULLTHUMPER II.

YOU'RE THE ONE WHO WANTS THAT GAME...

CLEAN OUT YOUR **OWN** CLOSET.

THE BOX! ≷PANT PANT≷ IS IT STILL FOR SALE?

HOW DID YOU GET HERE SO **QUICK?** I DIDN'T EVEN PUT AN ADDRESS IN MY POST.

UH...I'VE GOT A SPECIAL APP ON MY PHONE? ANYWAY, I'M WILLING TO PAY ONE HUNDRED DOLLARS FOR THAT BOX.

A HUNDRED DOLLARS?

YES! IN **REAL** MONEY!

I CAN DOUBLE WHATEVER THIS GUY IS OFFERING!!!

SHOVE

SLAM

SO DO WE HAVE A DEAL?

I DON'T KNOW IF—

MADAM! THERE IS NO NEED TO BE RUDE. I HAVE AS MUCH RIGHT TO DO BUSINESS HERE AS **ANY** WIZARD!

WIZARD?!

NOW, SIR. I'M SURE WE CAN COME TO AN **AGREEABLE ARRANGEMENT** IF YOU'LL GIVE ME A BALLPARK FIGURE.

WHAT DOES THE BOX EVEN DO?!

I'VE GOT TWO HUNDRED... DO I HEAR THREE?

WIZARDS THESE DAYS! RESORTING TO USING MONEY. HAVE YOU NO PRIDE?!

MY GOOD LAD, I'M PREPARED TO OFFER YOU ANY WISH YOUR HEART MIGHT DESIRE! PERHAPS A PET UNICORN?

DOES HE LOOK LIKE THE TYPE OF KID WHO WANTS A UNICORN?

I CAN MAKE YOU **TALLER**. AND GIVE YOU **BAT WINGS**! BOYS **LOVE** BAT WINGS.

THAT'S ENOUGH.

ZAP!

RIBBIT!

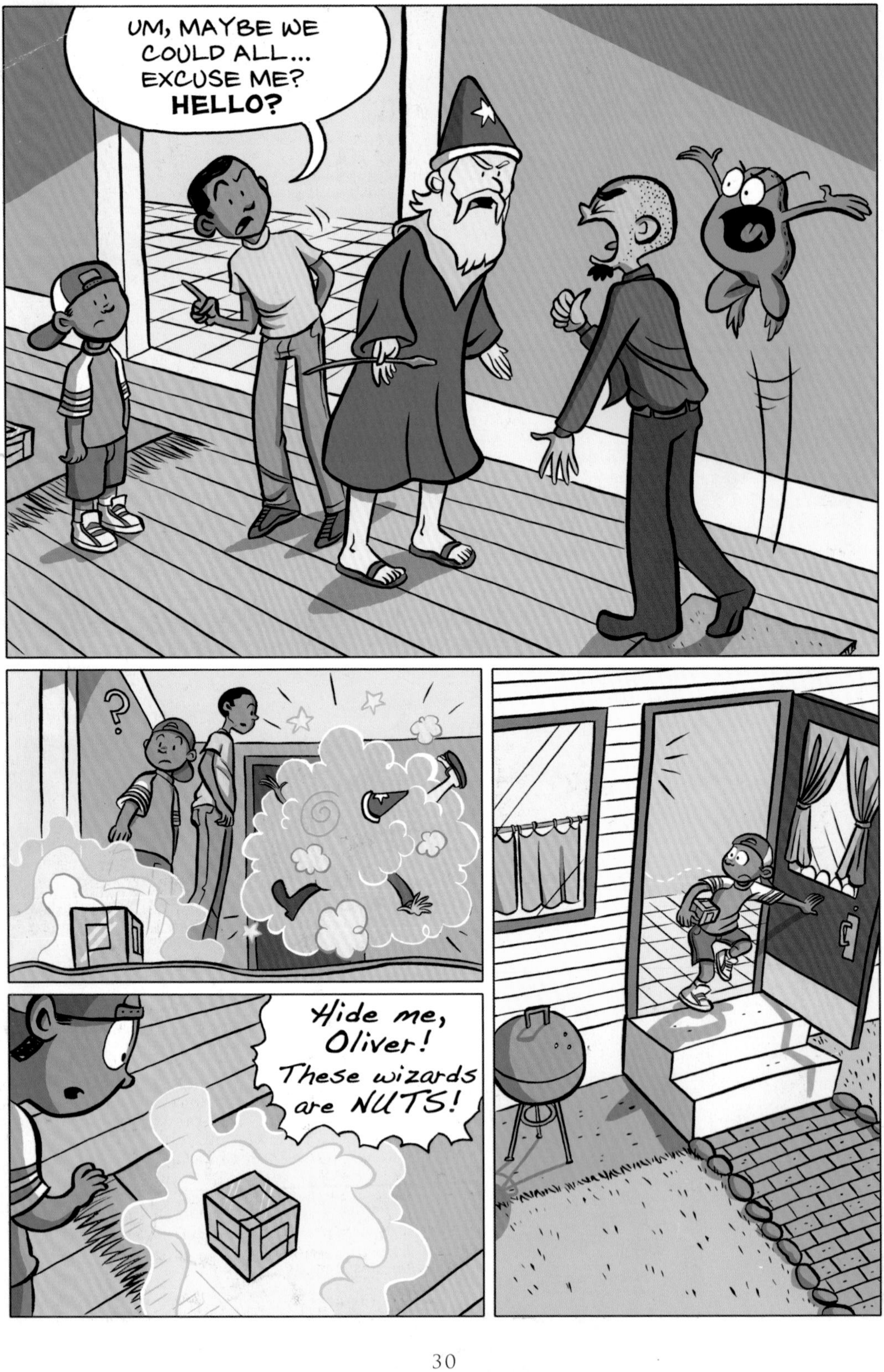
UM, MAYBE WE COULD ALL... EXCUSE ME? HELLO?
Hide me, Oliver! These wizards are NUTS!

MIND IF I TAKE A CLOSER LOOK?

I'M NOT SURE IF...

YOU CAN **TRUST** ME. I'M AN EXPERT AT THESE TYPES OF THINGS.

MY PARENTS THINK I'M CRAZY, BUT I PLAN TO MAJOR IN ADVANCED MYSTICAL RESEARCH WHEN I GO TO COLLEGE.

?

HOW DID THOSE WIZARDS FIND ME?

YOU CAN'T PUT MAGICAL OBJECTS ON THE INTERNET WITHOUT STUFF LIKE THIS HAPPENING.

A LOT OF WIZARDS TROLL AROUND, WAITING FOR LOST ARTIFACTS TO REVEAL THEMSELVES.

Typey Type Type

MY GUESS IS THAT YOUR BOX IS ONE OF THESE.

Ancient Transport

Instant Death

"ENCHANTED WITH LIVING MAGIC, SORCERERS USE THEM TO CROSS INTO VARIOUS DIMENSIONS."

A BOX ONLY WORKS WITH ITS PARTNER. SUPPOSEDLY, THESE MATCHING SETS WERE ALL SCATTERED AND LOST DURING SOME WIZARD WAR BACK IN THE DAY.

POOR THING. ALL THESE YEARS, TRAPPED IN OUR WORLD.

ALL HE WANTS IS A SAFE PLACE TO REST.

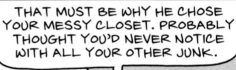

THAT MUST BE WHY HE CHOSE YOUR MESSY CLOSET. PROBABLY THOUGHT YOU'D NEVER NOTICE WITH ALL YOUR OTHER JUNK.

IT'S A **GIRL.**

HOW CAN YOU TELL?

I HEARD HER VOICE IN MY **HEAD.**

SHE KNOWS MY NAME!

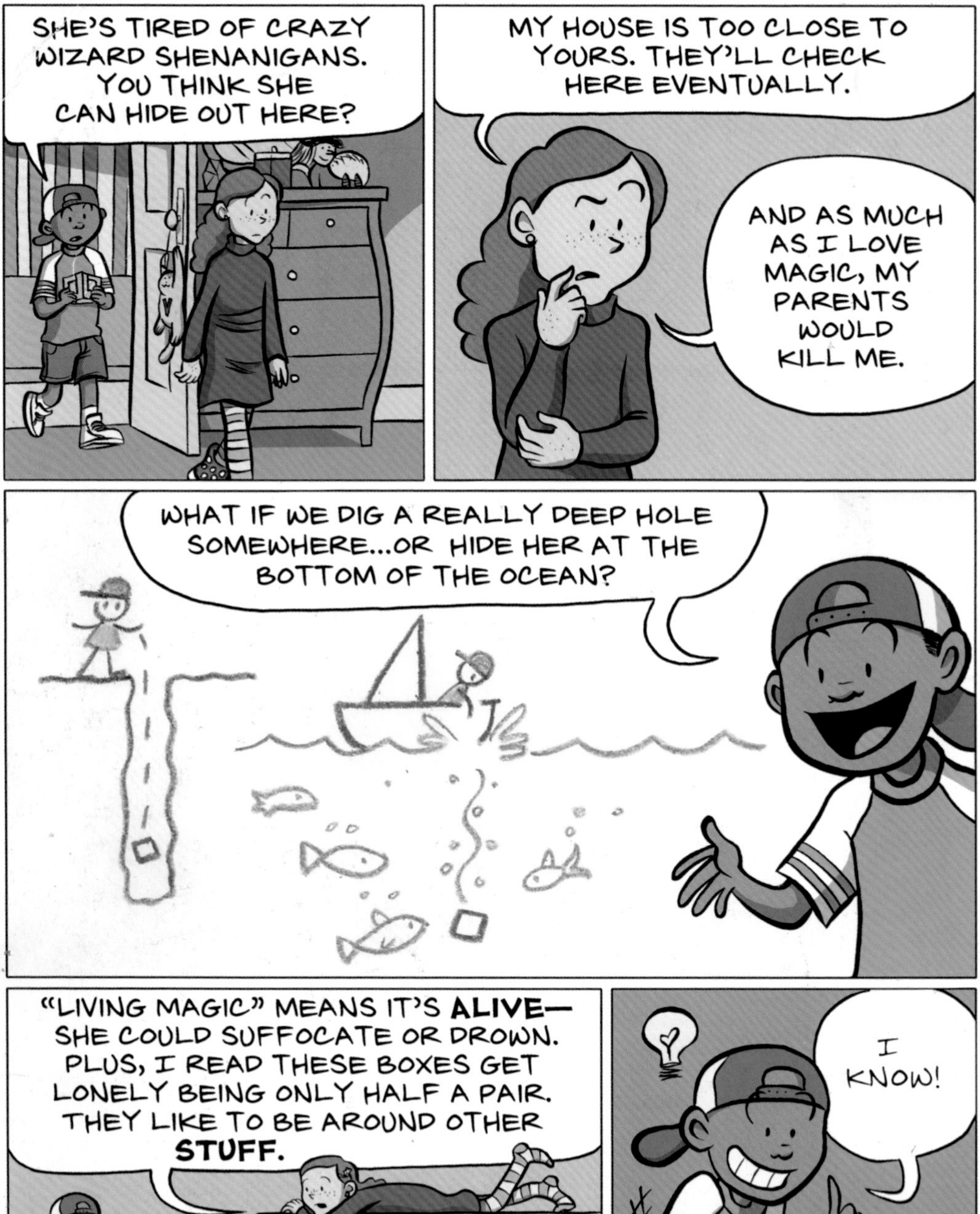
SHE'S TIRED OF CRAZY WIZARD SHENANIGANS. YOU THINK SHE CAN HIDE OUT HERE?
MY HOUSE IS TOO CLOSE TO YOURS. THEY'LL CHECK HERE EVENTUALLY.
AND AS MUCH AS I LOVE MAGIC, MY PARENTS WOULD KILL ME.
WHAT IF WE DIG A REALLY DEEP HOLE SOMEWHERE...OR HIDE HER AT THE BOTTOM OF THE OCEAN?
"LIVING MAGIC" MEANS IT'S **ALIVE**—SHE COULD SUFFOCATE OR DROWN. PLUS, I READ THESE BOXES GET LONELY BEING ONLY HALF A PAIR. THEY LIKE TO BE AROUND OTHER **STUFF**.
WHAT ABOUT A MUSEUM? OR AN ANTIQUES STORE?
I KNOW!

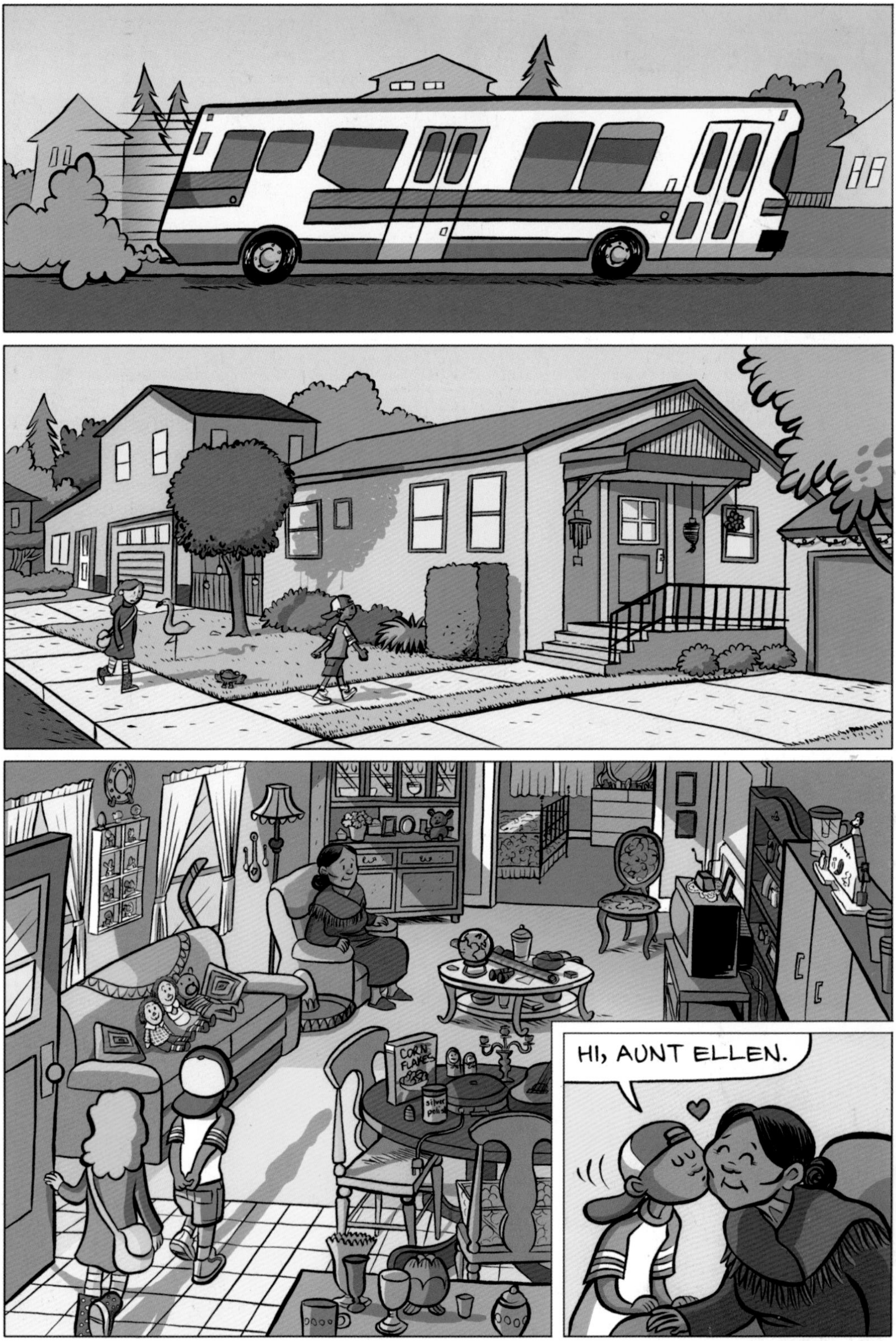
HI, AUNT ELLEN.
CORN FLAKES

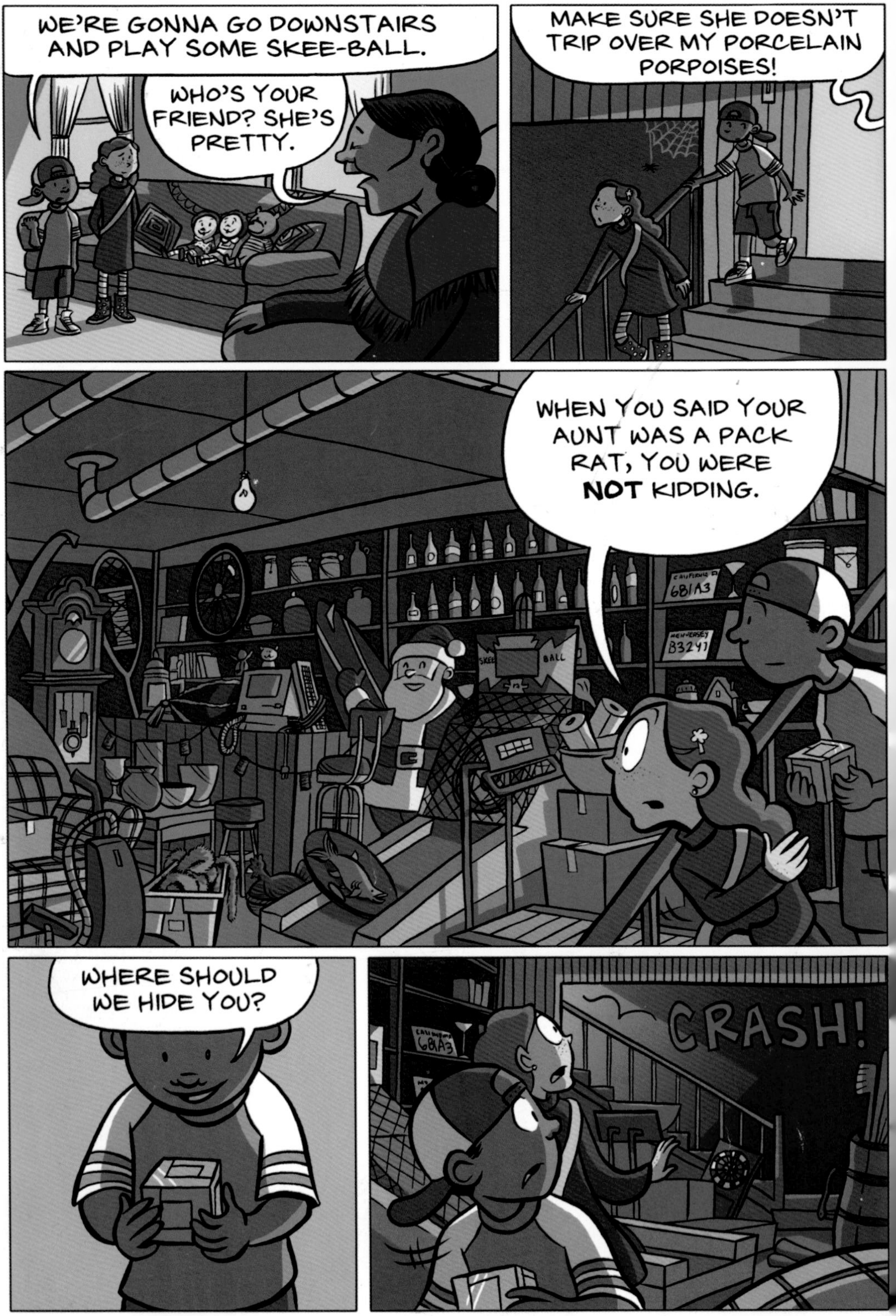
WE'RE GONNA GO DOWNSTAIRS AND PLAY SOME SKEE-BALL.
WHO'S YOUR FRIEND? SHE'S PRETTY.
MAKE SURE SHE DOESN'T TRIP OVER MY PORCELAIN PORPOISES!
WHEN YOU SAID YOUR AUNT WAS A PACK RAT, YOU WERE **NOT** KIDDING.
WHERE SHOULD WE HIDE YOU?
CRASH!

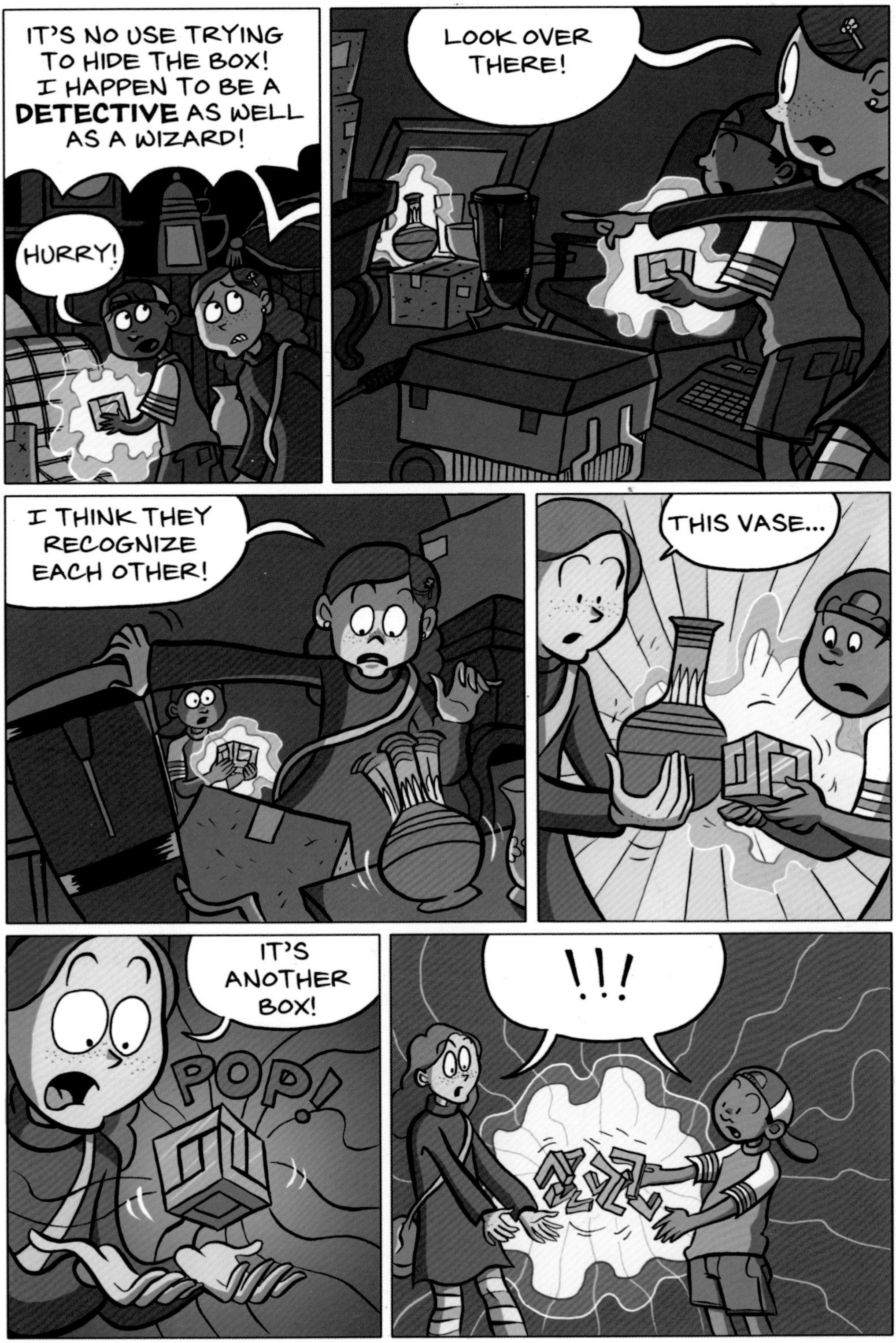
IT'S NO USE TRYING TO HIDE THE BOX! I HAPPEN TO BE A **DETECTIVE** AS WELL AS A WIZARD!
HURRY!
LOOK OVER THERE!
I THINK THEY RECOGNIZE EACH OTHER!
THIS VASE...
IT'S ANOTHER BOX!
POP!
!!!

My love! I'd lost hope of ever finding you again!

Thank you, Oliver and Valerie! Thank you both!

VOOOSH

POOF!

WHAT JUST HAPPENED?

THEY COMBINED POWERS TO MOVE TO ANOTHER DIMENSION WHERE THEY CAN HIDE TOGETHER?

JUST A THEORY.

THUMP

HMPH! CHILDREN, DO YOU KNOW THESE CHARACTERS?

NOT INTENTIONALLY.

THE END!

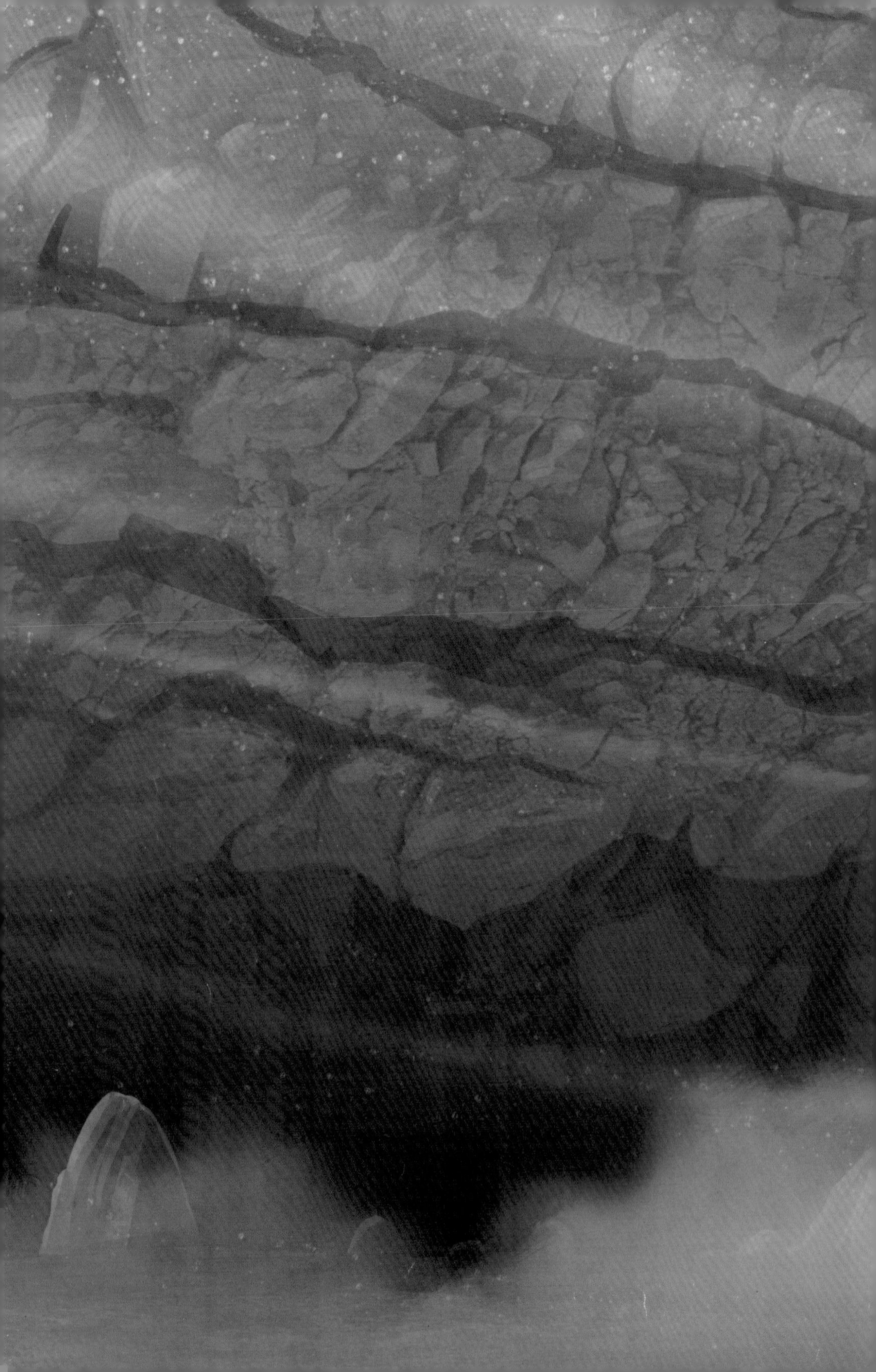

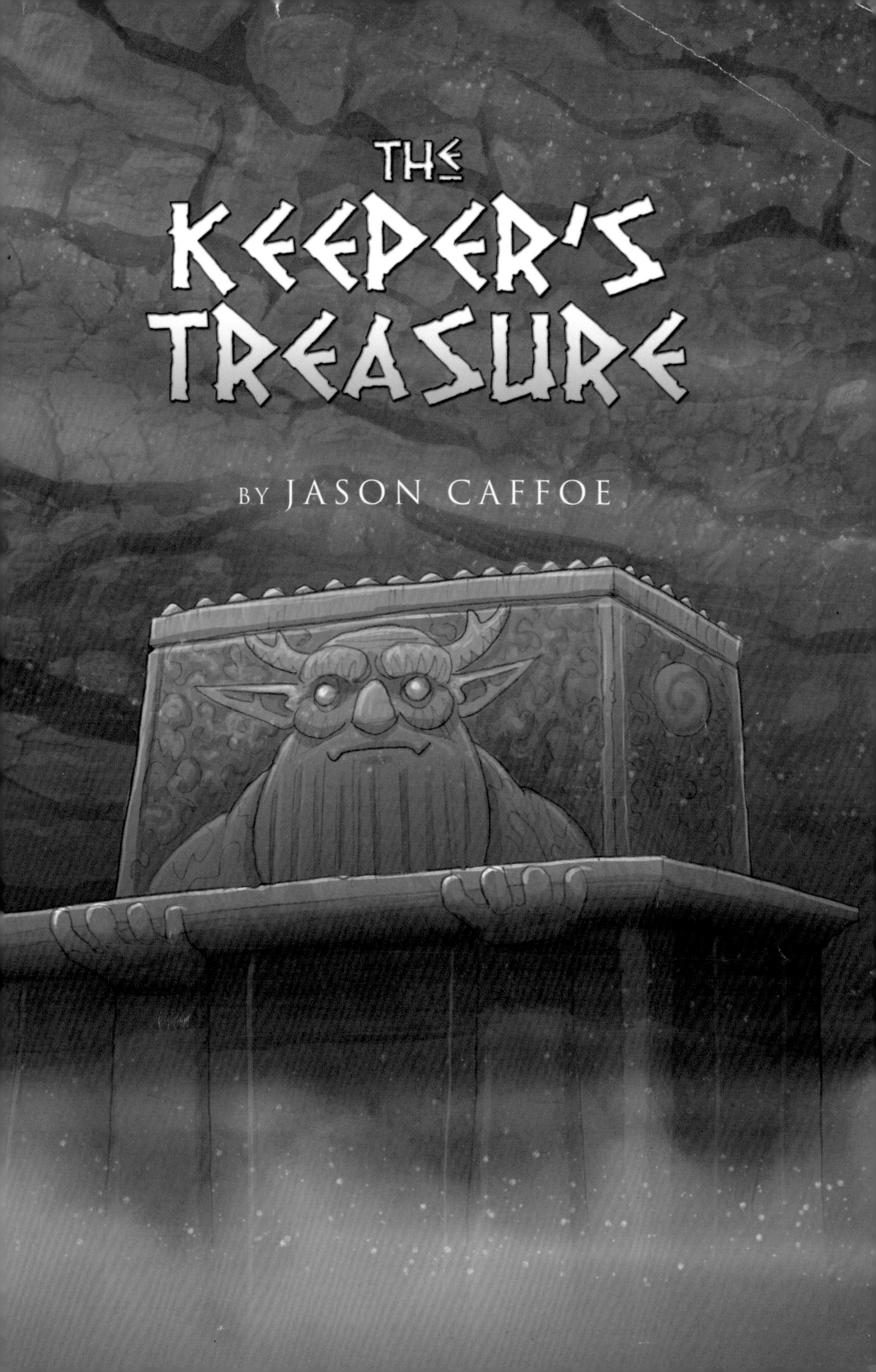
THE
KEEPER'S
TREASURE
BY JASON CAFFOE

SIGH...

I CAN'T BELIEVE THIS.

TREASURE HERE

OF COURSE THIS STUPID PLACE ISN'T ON THE MAP.

WHY WOULD IT BE?

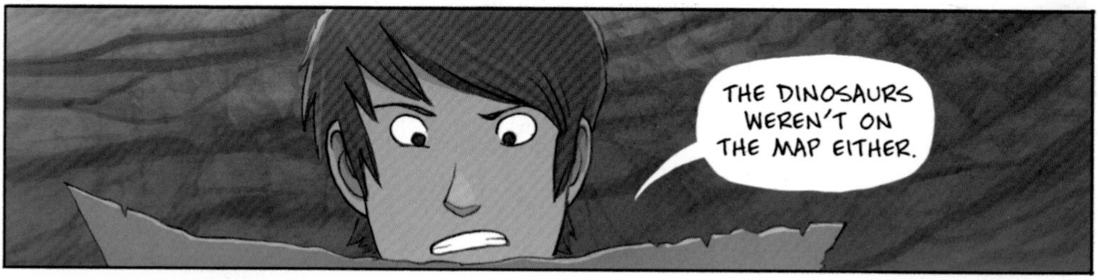
THE DINOSAURS WEREN'T ON THE MAP EITHER.

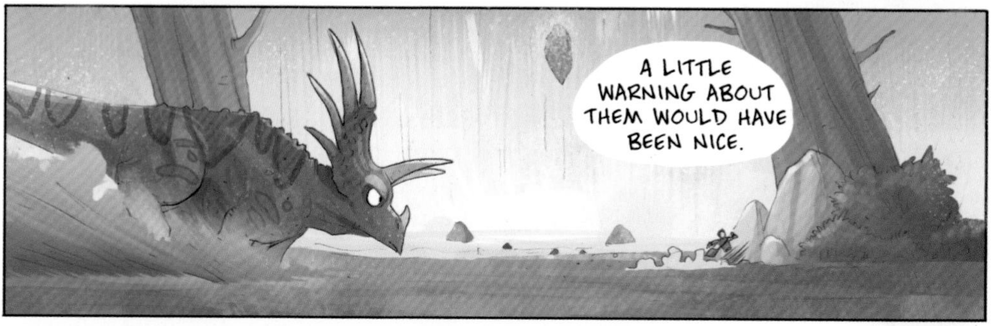
A LITTLE WARNING ABOUT THEM WOULD HAVE BEEN NICE.

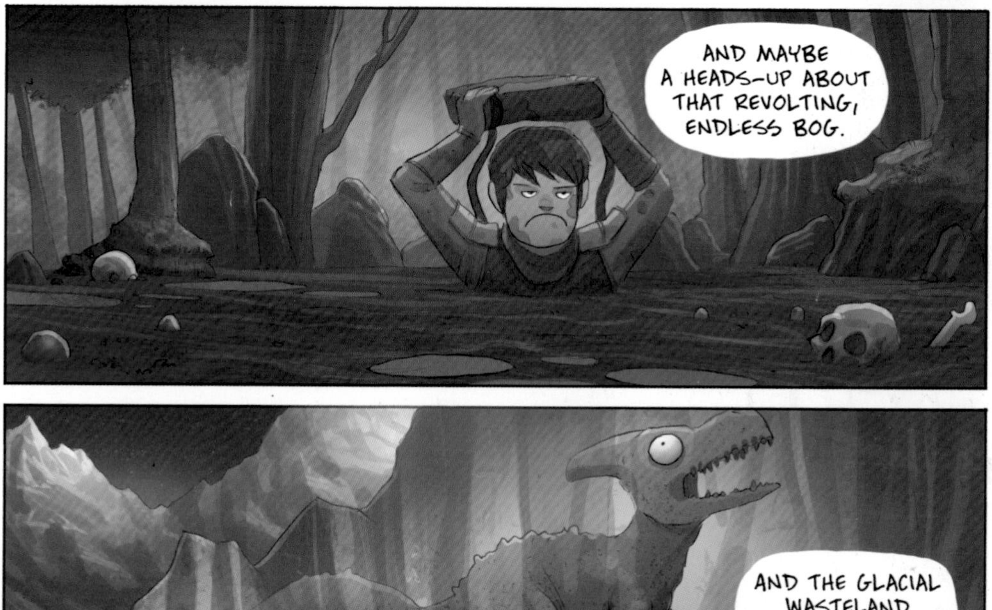
AND MAYBE A HEADS-UP ABOUT THAT REVOLTING, ENDLESS BOG.

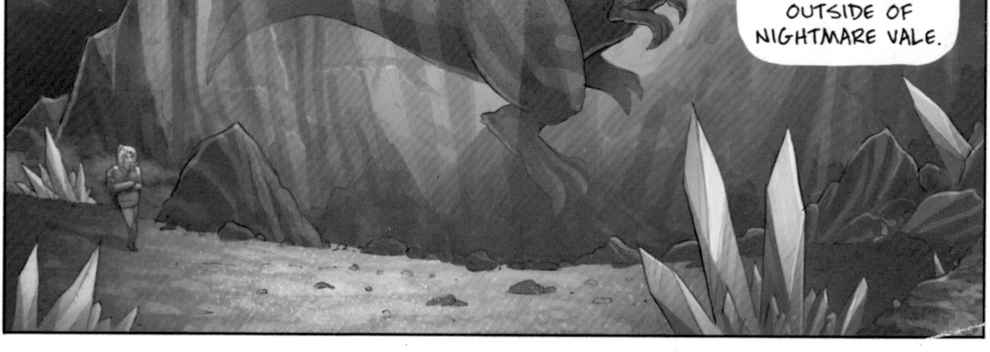
AND THE GLACIAL WASTELAND OUTSIDE OF NIGHTMARE VALE.

AND THEN, AFTER ALL THAT, I FINALLY REACH THIS TEMPLE,

AND I THINK MY TROUBLES ARE OVER!

TREASURE HERE

OH WAIT, THERE'S AN ENDLESS, EMPTY LABYRINTH INSIDE.

MIGHT'VE BEEN NICE TO HAVE SEEN THAT ON THE MAP, TOO.

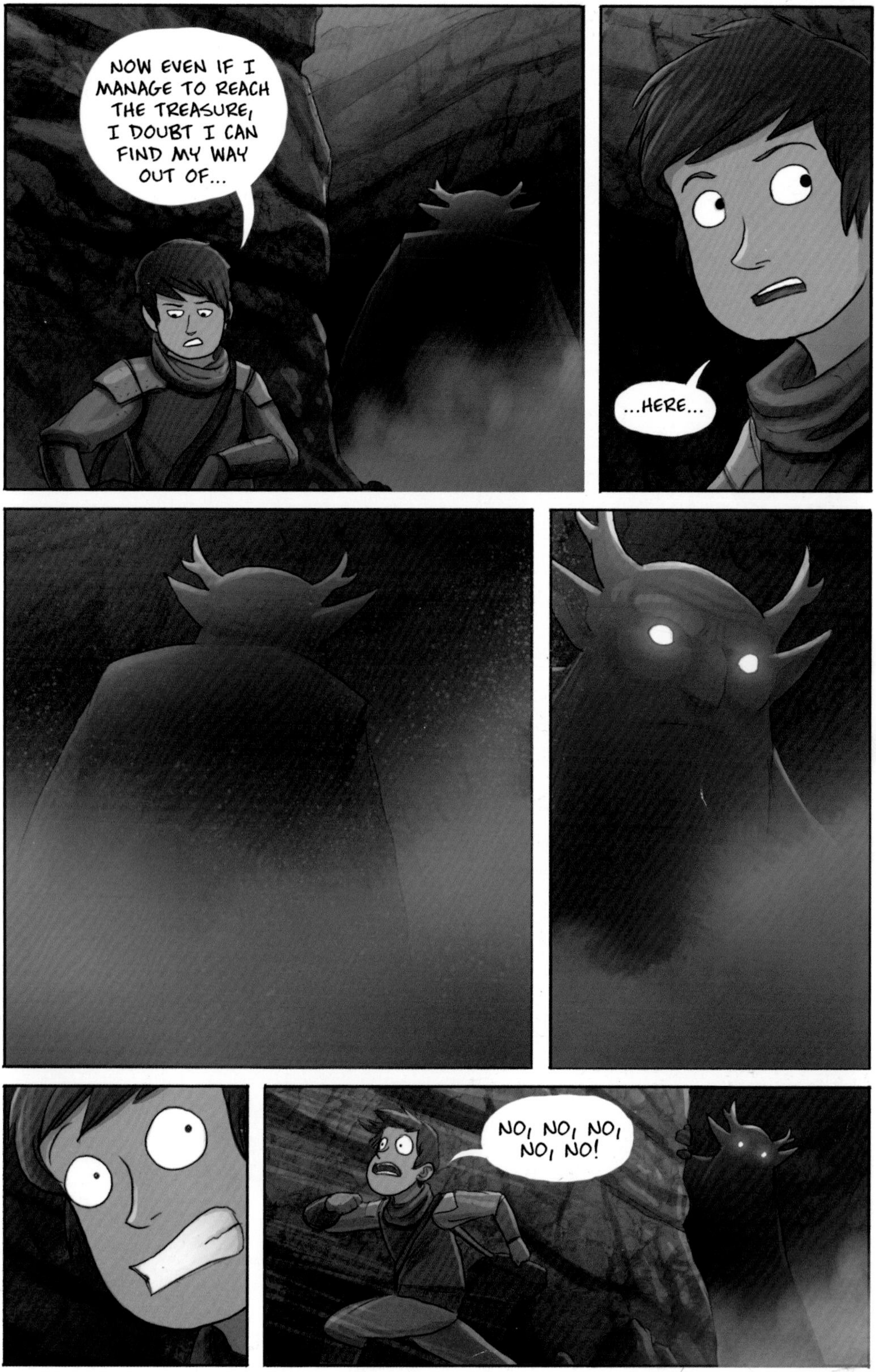
NOW EVEN IF I MANAGE TO REACH THE TREASURE, I DOUBT I CAN FIND MY WAY OUT OF...
...HERE...
NO, NO, NO, NO, NO!

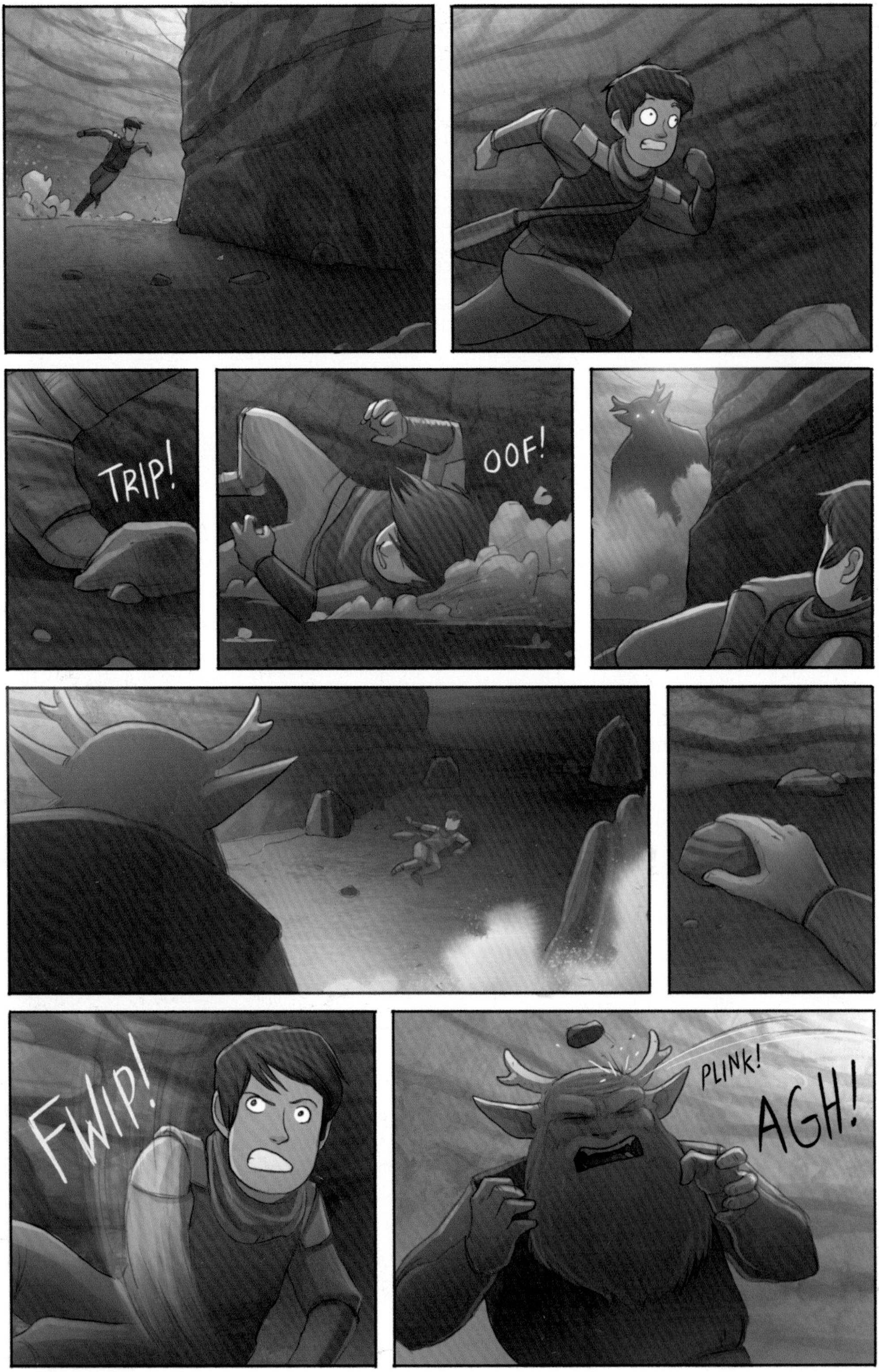
TRIP!
OOF!
FWIP!
PLINK!
AGH!

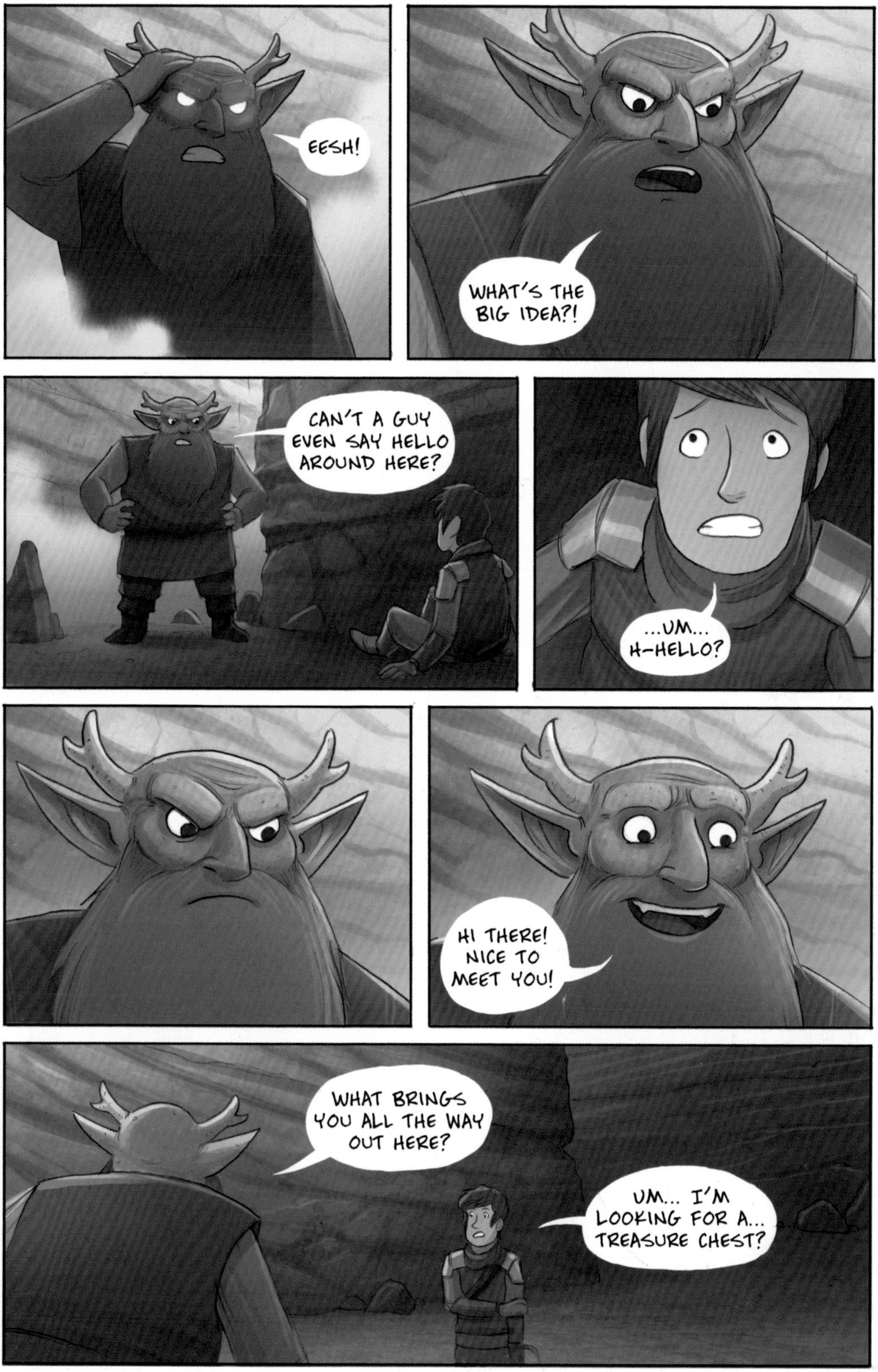
EESH!
WHAT'S THE BIG IDEA?!
CAN'T A GUY EVEN SAY HELLO AROUND HERE?
...UM... H-HELLO?
HI THERE! NICE TO MEET YOU!
WHAT BRINGS YOU ALL THE WAY OUT HERE?
UM... I'M LOOKING FOR A... TREASURE CHEST?

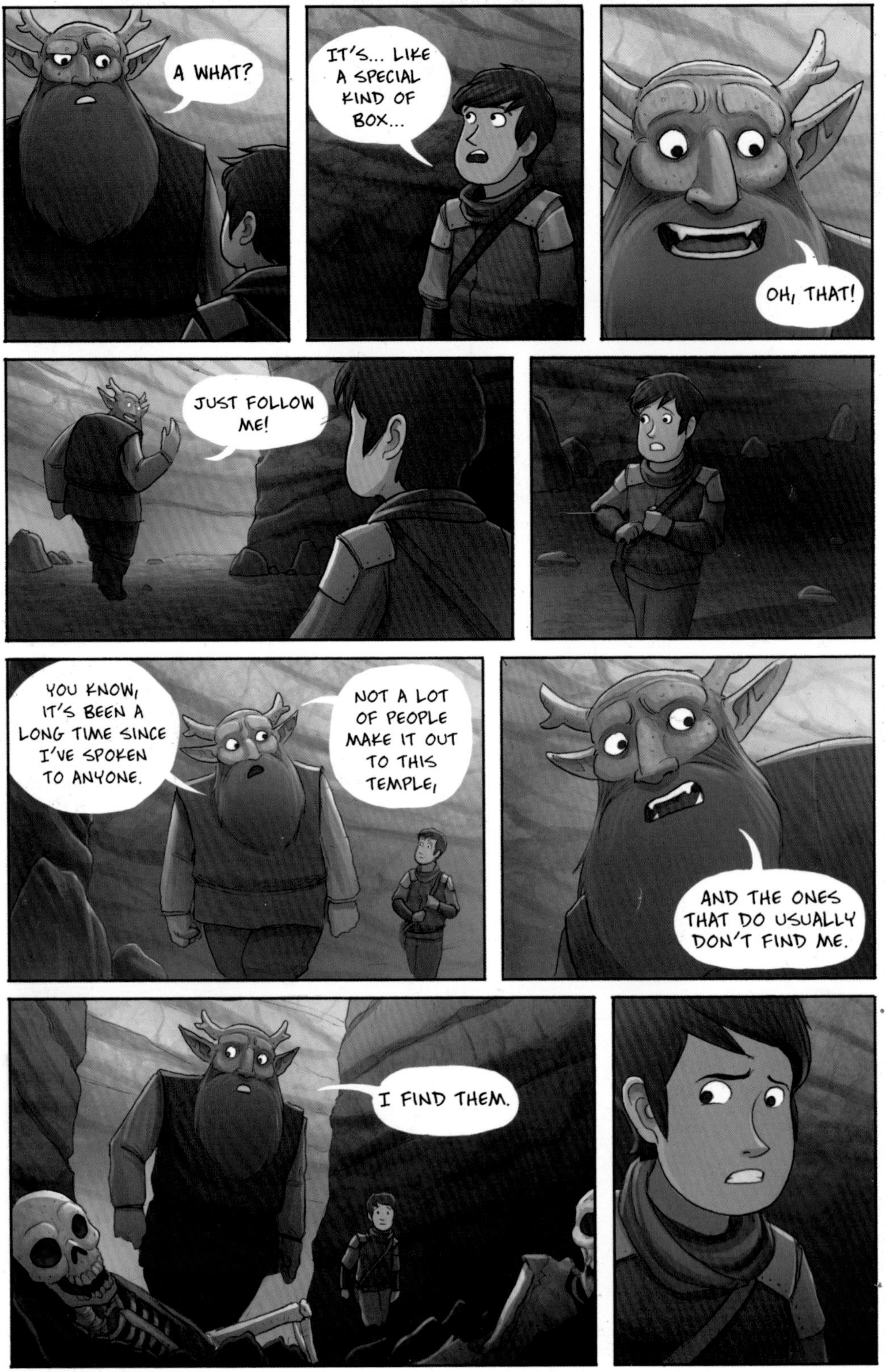
A WHAT?
IT'S... LIKE A SPECIAL KIND OF BOX...
OH, THAT!
JUST FOLLOW ME!
YOU KNOW, IT'S BEEN A LONG TIME SINCE I'VE SPOKEN TO ANYONE.
NOT A LOT OF PEOPLE MAKE IT OUT TO THIS TEMPLE,
AND THE ONES THAT DO USUALLY DON'T FIND ME.
I FIND THEM.

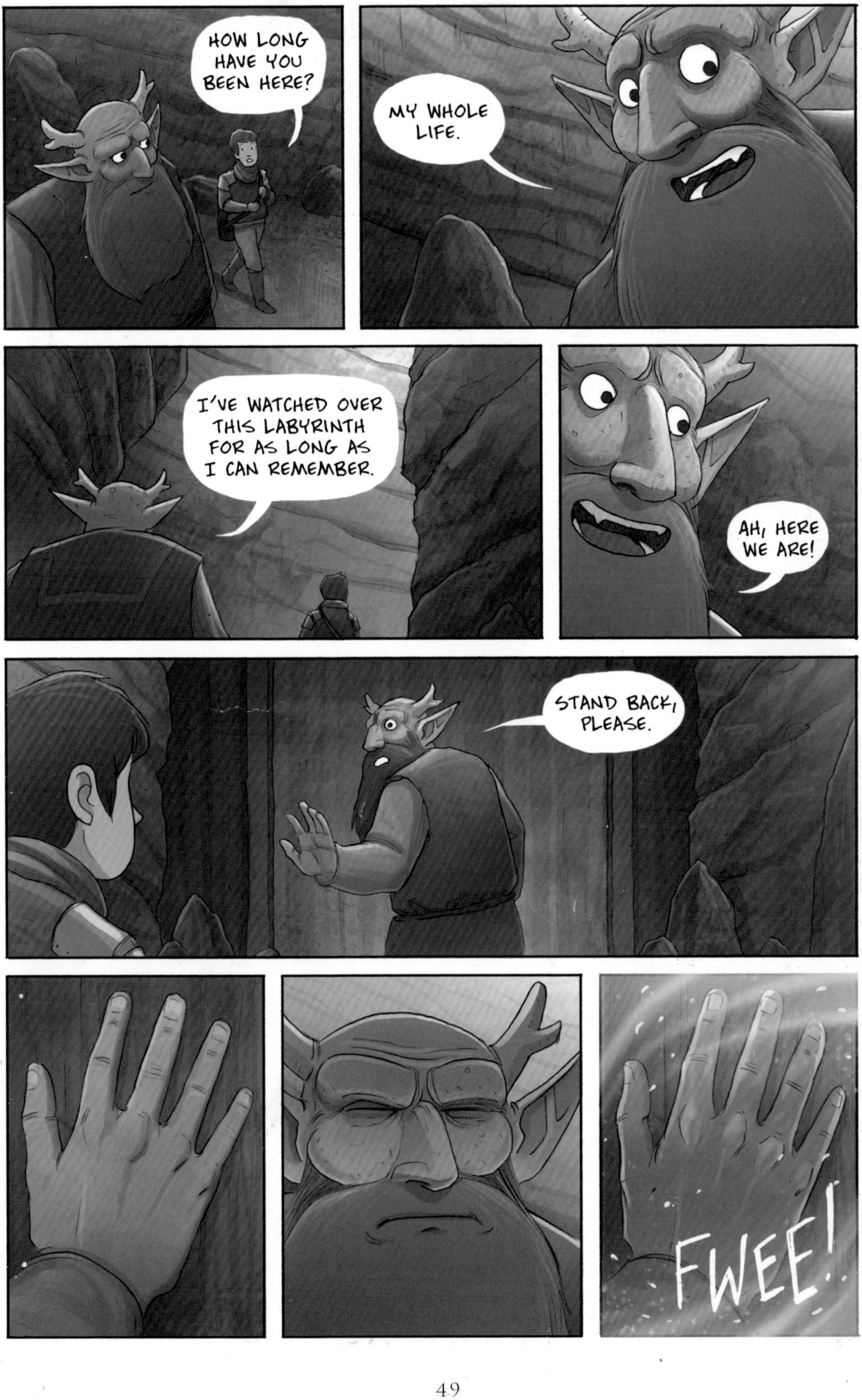
HOW LONG HAVE YOU BEEN HERE?
MY WHOLE LIFE.
I'VE WATCHED OVER THIS LABYRINTH FOR AS LONG AS I CAN REMEMBER.
AH, HERE WE ARE!
STAND BACK, PLEASE.
FWEE!

WHAT'S IN IT?

I ACTUALLY DON'T KNOW,

BUT IT'S MY FAVORITE THING IN THE TEMPLE.

HAVEN'T YOU EVER WONDERED WHAT'S INSIDE?

OF COURSE!

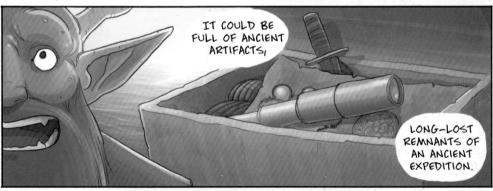

IT COULD BE FULL OF ANCIENT ARTIFACTS,

LONG-LOST REMNANTS OF AN ANCIENT EXPEDITION.

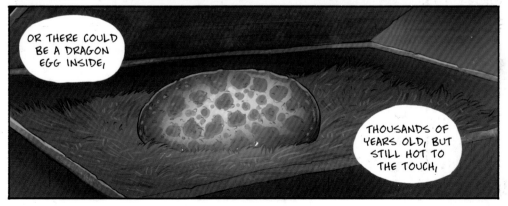

OR THERE COULD BE A DRAGON EGG INSIDE,

THOUSANDS OF YEARS OLD, BUT STILL HOT TO THE TOUCH,

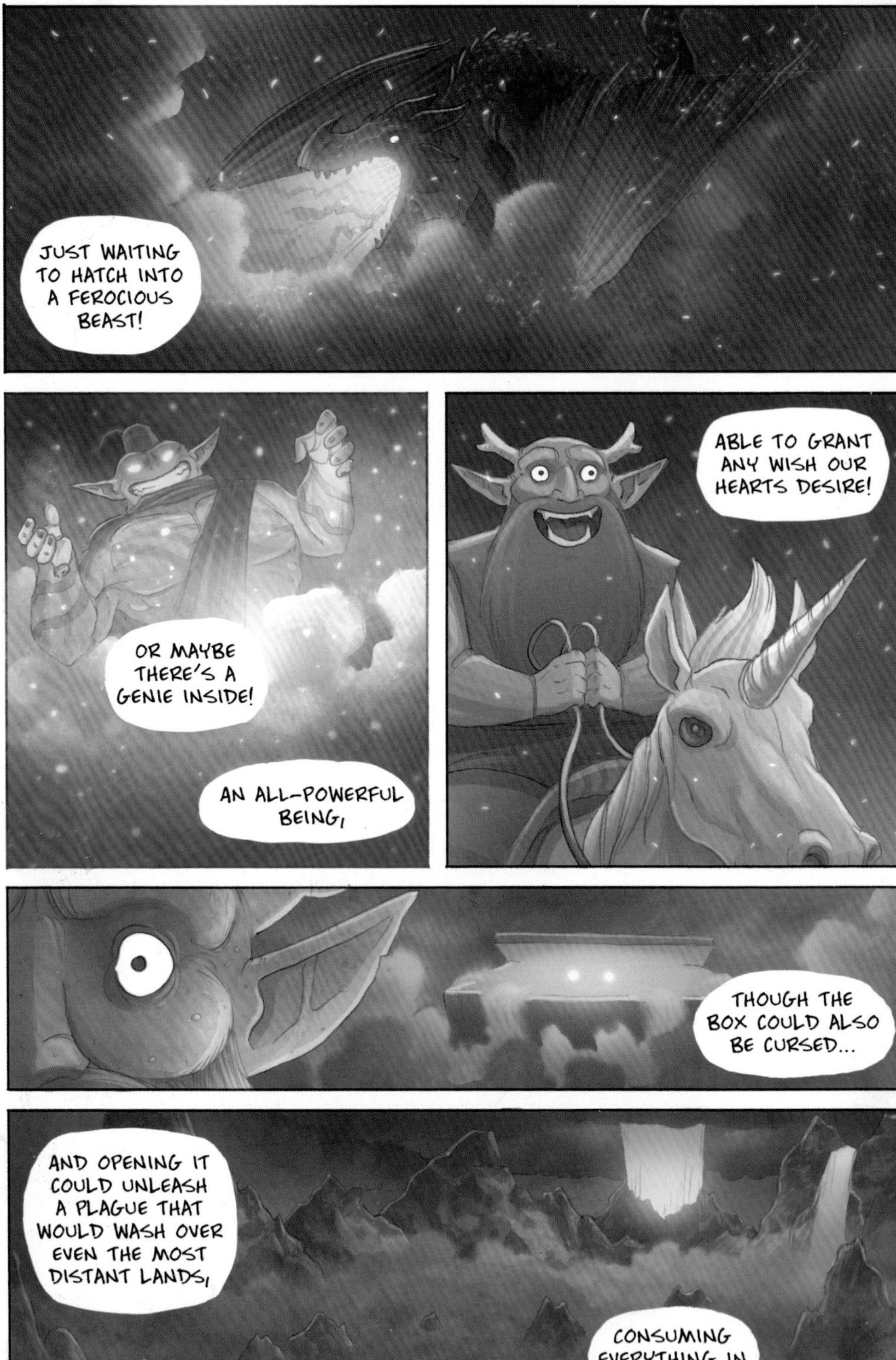
JUST WAITING TO HATCH INTO A FEROCIOUS BEAST!
OR MAYBE THERE'S A GENIE INSIDE!
AN ALL-POWERFUL BEING,
ABLE TO GRANT ANY WISH OUR HEARTS DESIRE!
THOUGH THE BOX COULD ALSO BE CURSED...
AND OPENING IT COULD UNLEASH A PLAGUE THAT WOULD WASH OVER EVEN THE MOST DISTANT LANDS,
CONSUMING EVERYTHING IN ITS PATH.

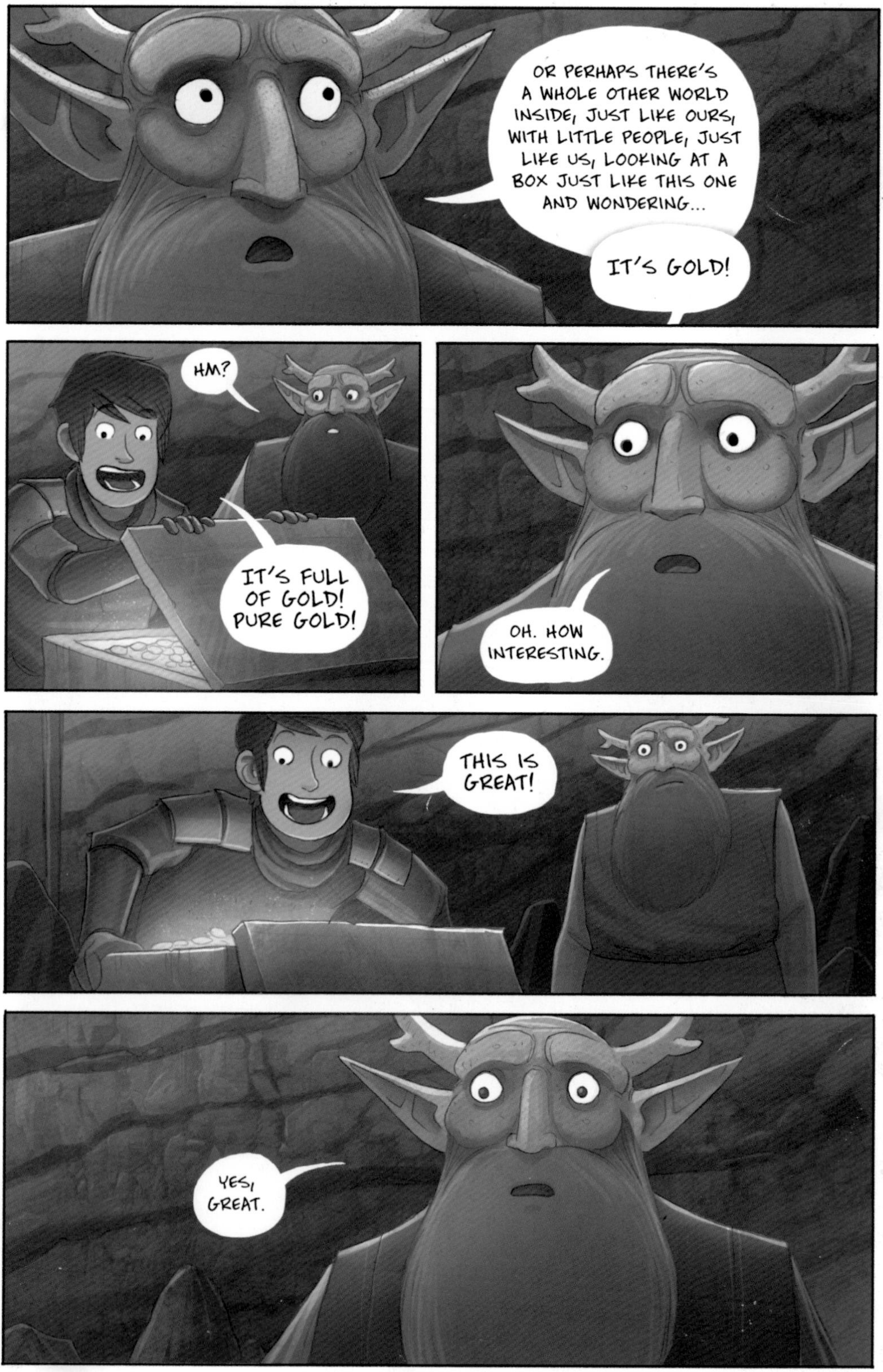
OR PERHAPS THERE'S A WHOLE OTHER WORLD INSIDE, JUST LIKE OURS, WITH LITTLE PEOPLE, JUST LIKE US, LOOKING AT A BOX JUST LIKE THIS ONE AND WONDERING...
IT'S GOLD!
HM?
IT'S FULL OF GOLD! PURE GOLD!
OH. HOW INTERESTING.
THIS IS GREAT!
YES, GREAT.

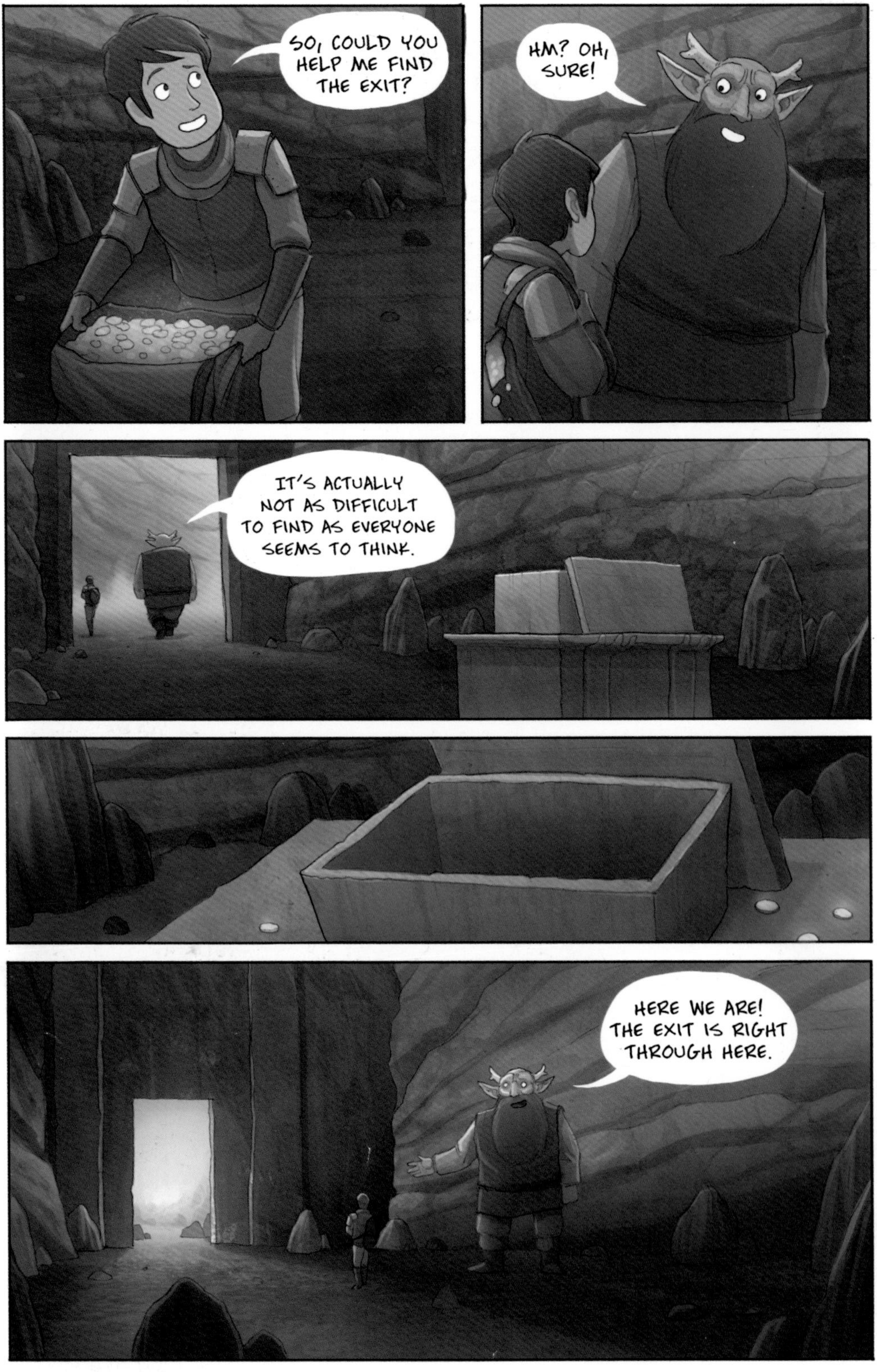
SO, COULD YOU HELP ME FIND THE EXIT?
HM? OH, SURE!
IT'S ACTUALLY NOT AS DIFFICULT TO FIND AS EVERYONE SEEMS TO THINK.
HERE WE ARE! THE EXIT IS RIGHT THROUGH HERE.

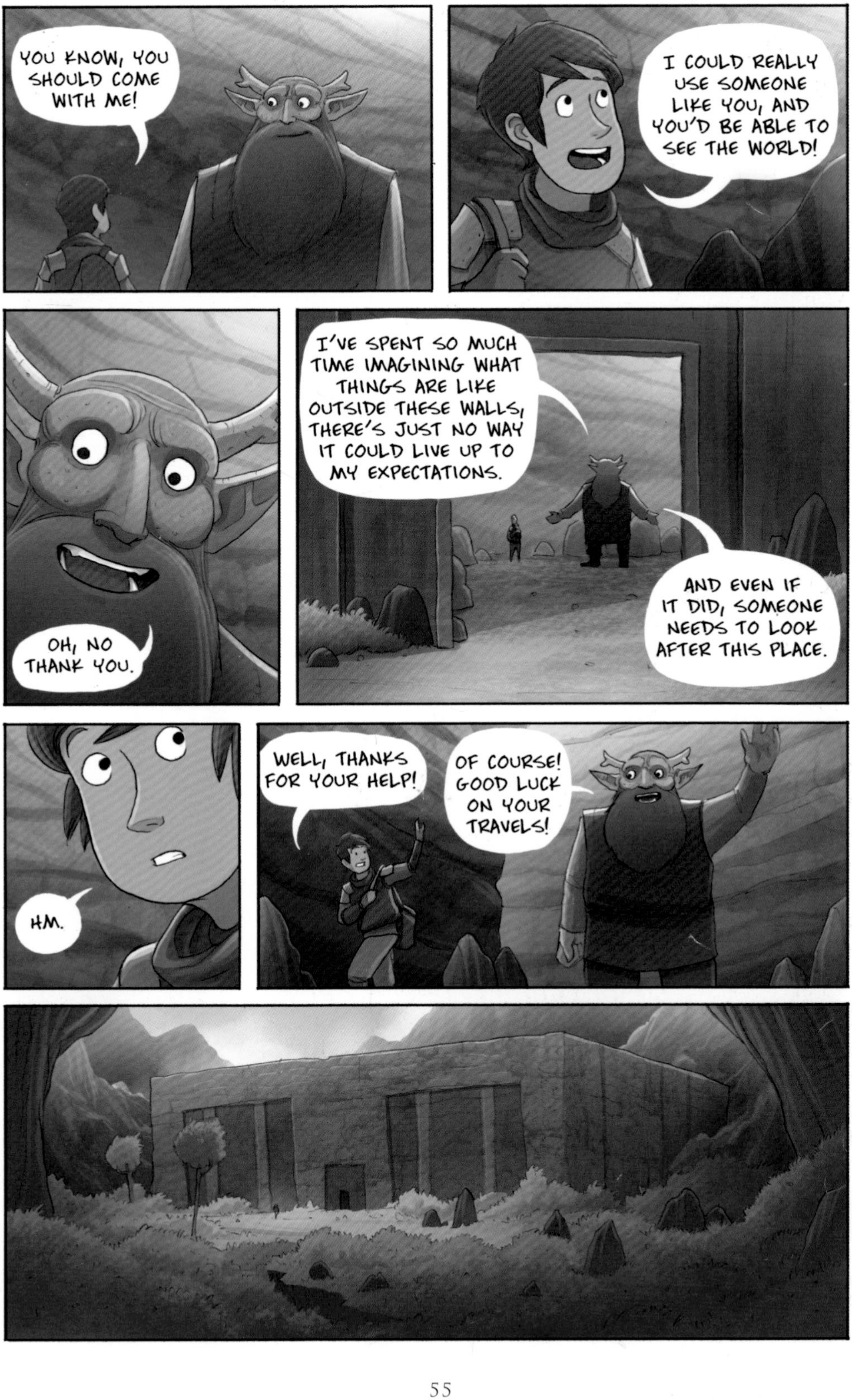
YOU KNOW, YOU SHOULD COME WITH ME!
I COULD REALLY USE SOMEONE LIKE YOU, AND YOU'D BE ABLE TO SEE THE WORLD!
OH, NO THANK YOU.
I'VE SPENT SO MUCH TIME IMAGINING WHAT THINGS ARE LIKE OUTSIDE THESE WALLS, THERE'S JUST NO WAY IT COULD LIVE UP TO MY EXPECTATIONS.
AND EVEN IF IT DID, SOMEONE NEEDS TO LOOK AFTER THIS PLACE.
HM.
WELL, THANKS FOR YOUR HELP!
OF COURSE! GOOD LUCK ON YOUR TRAVELS!

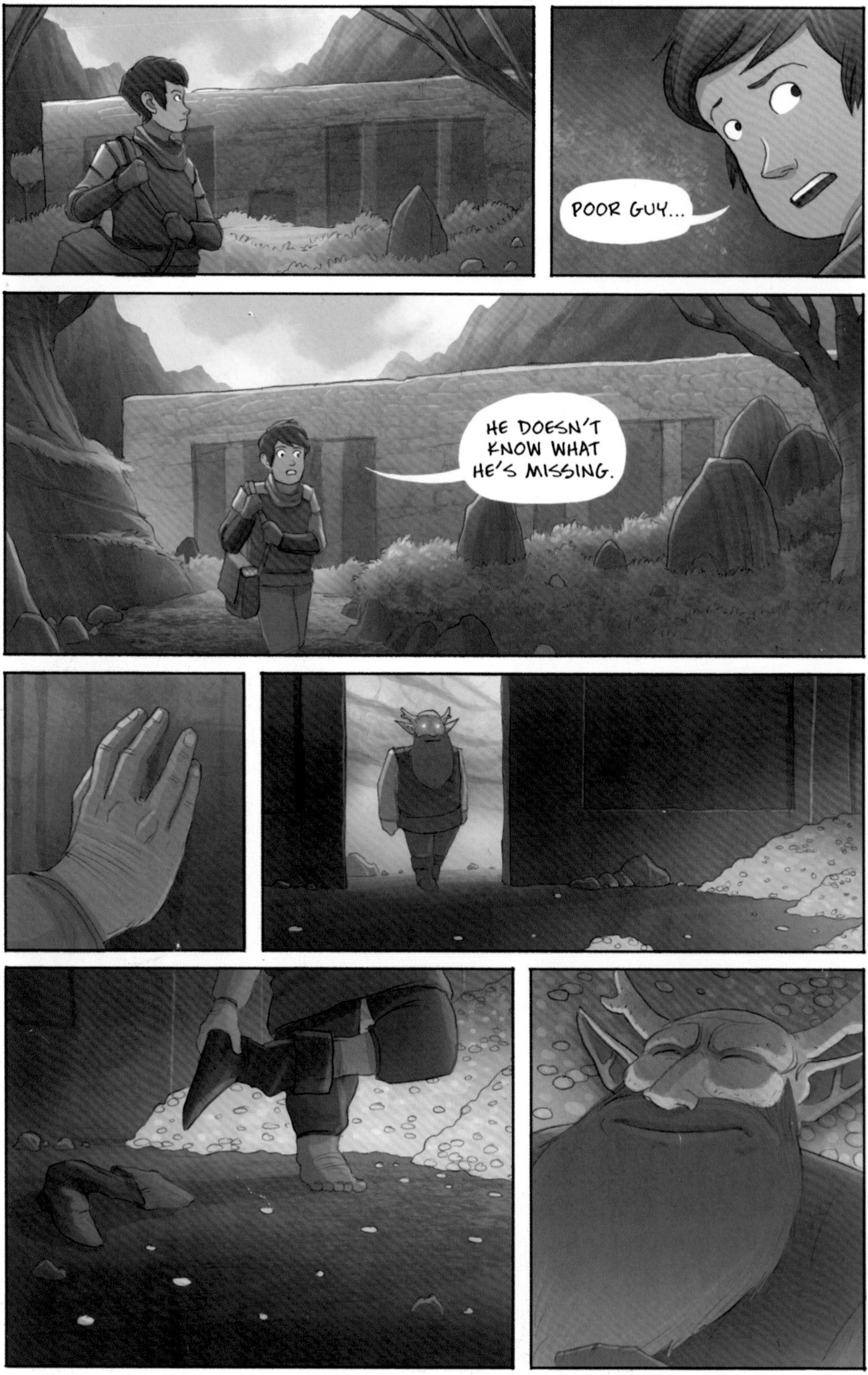
POOR GUY...
HE DOESN'T KNOW WHAT HE'S MISSING.

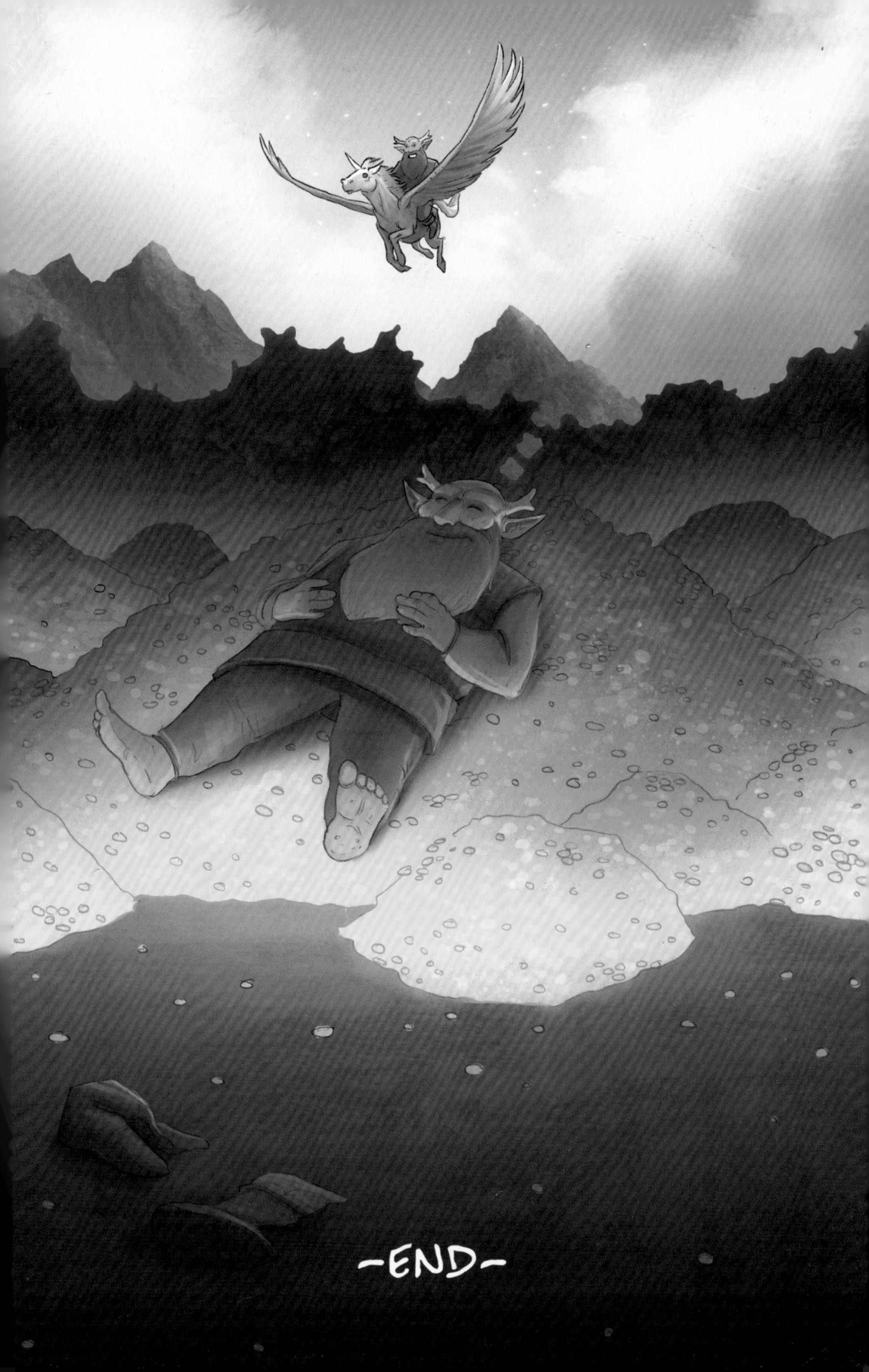
-END-

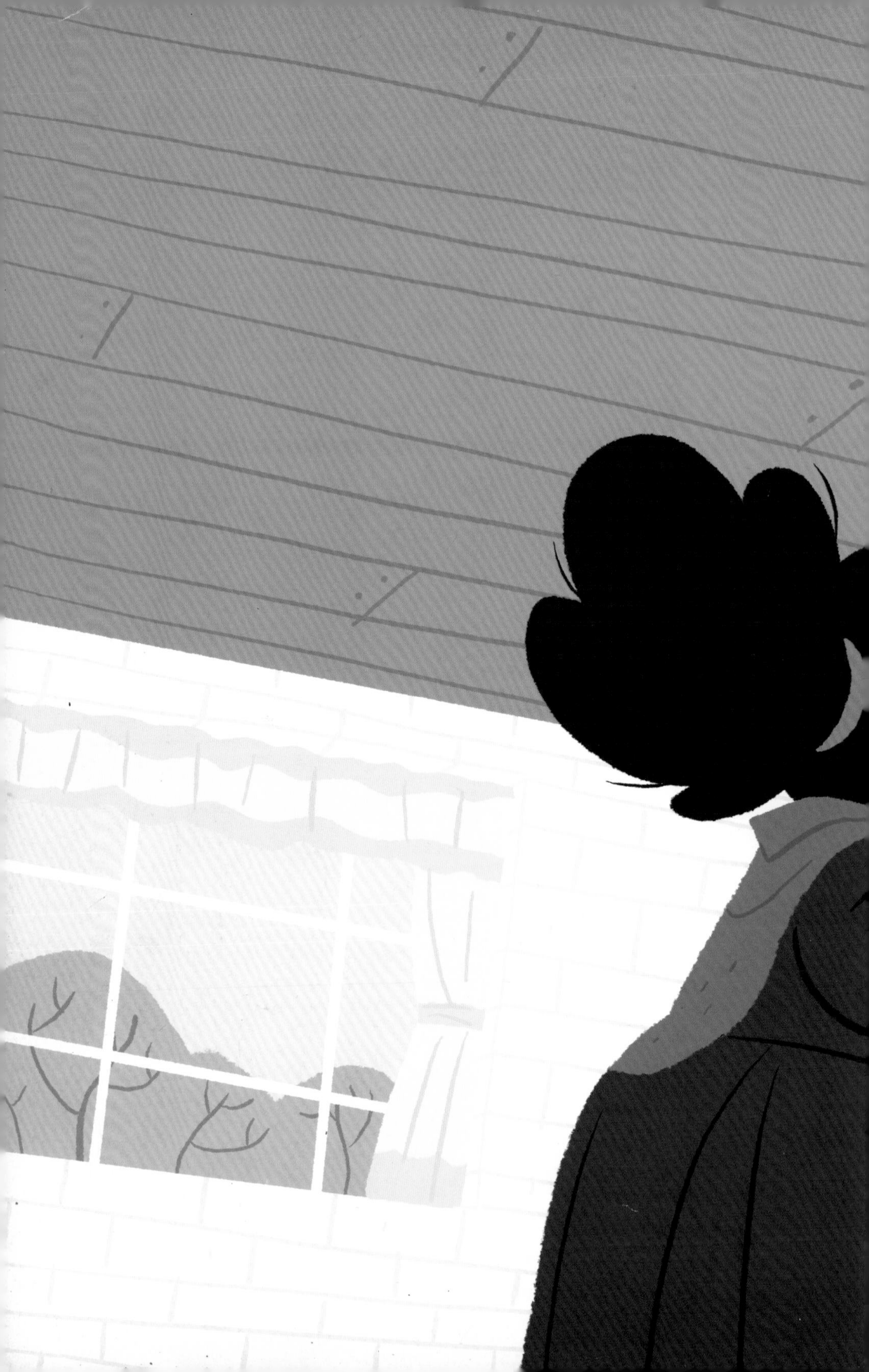

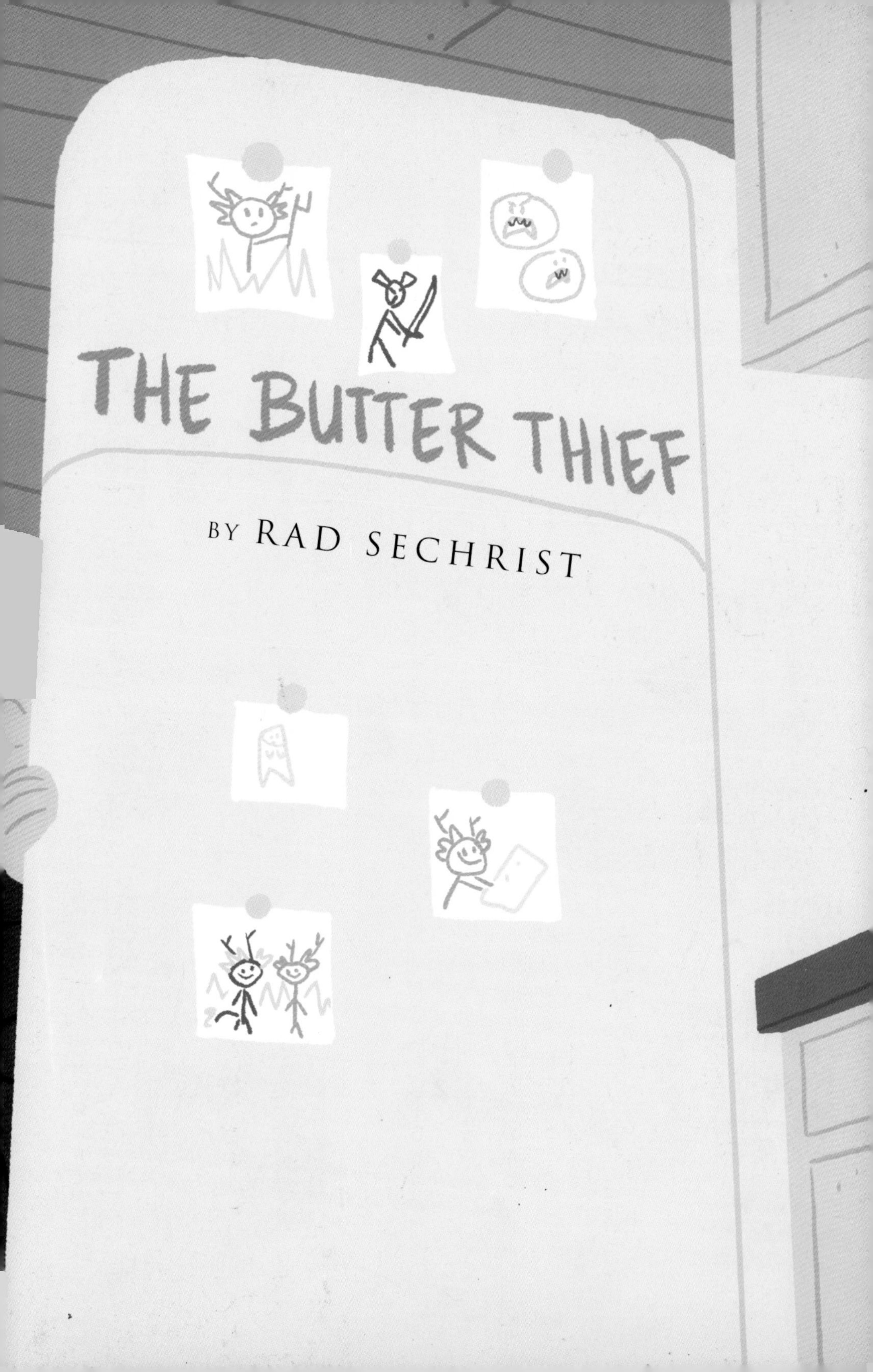
THE BUTTER THIEF
BY RAD SECHRIST

MOM...

呪われ

WHAT'S GRANDMA DOING?

竹箱の 中に

SIGH... SHE THINKS THERE'S A SPIRIT STEALING BUTTER FROM THE FRIDGE...

永遠に

AND SHE'S TRYING TO TRAP IT.

OBAASAN! THERE IS NO SPIRIT...

閉じ込む わべし!!

STEALING BUTTER—

SNAP!

あっ

SHE SAYS
SHE CAUGHT
IT.

捕
え
た
か
の
う

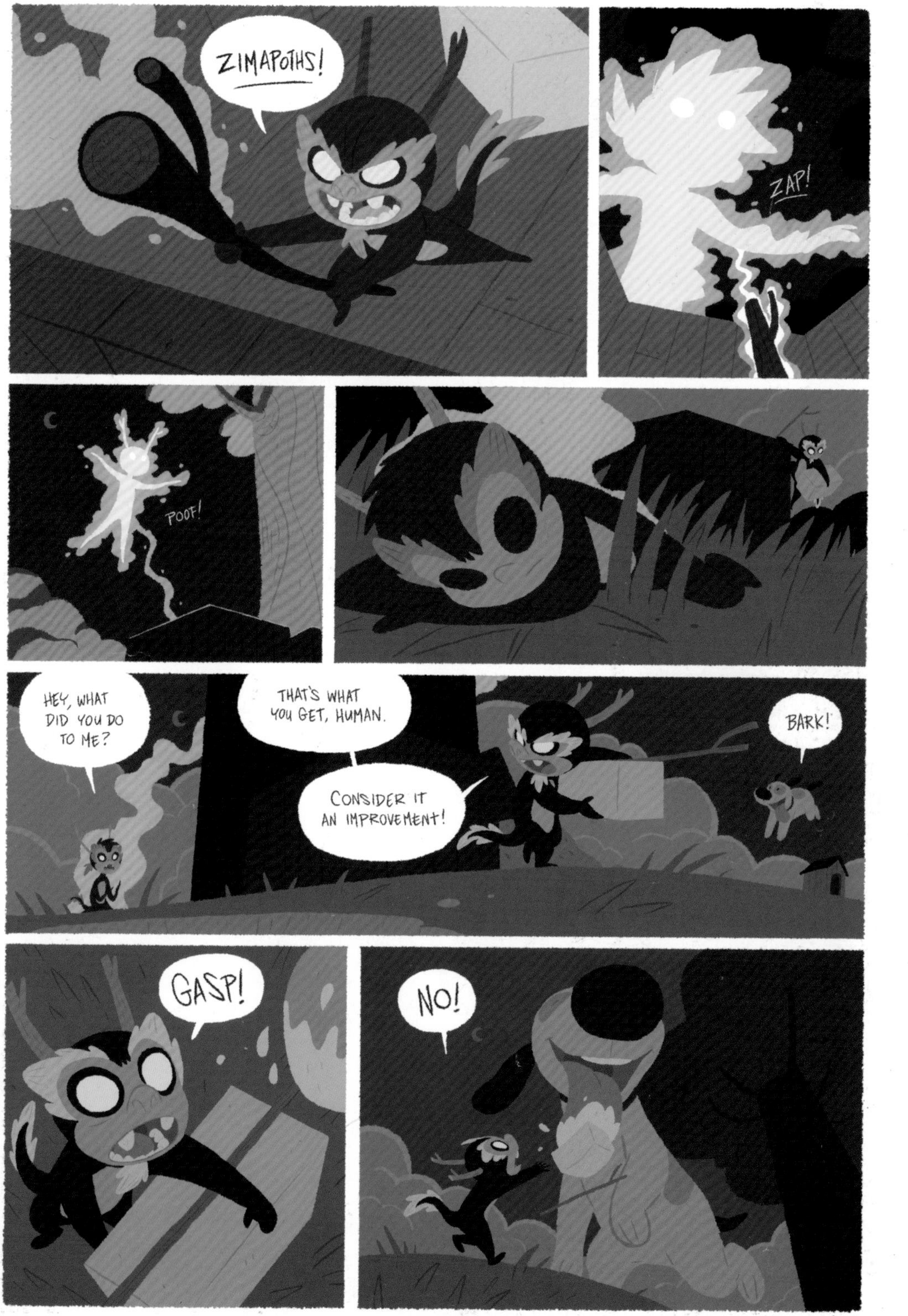
ZIMAPOTHS!
ZAP!
POOF!
HEY, WHAT DID YOU DO TO ME?
THAT'S WHAT YOU GET, HUMAN.
CONSIDER IT AN IMPROVEMENT!
BARK!
GASP!
NO!

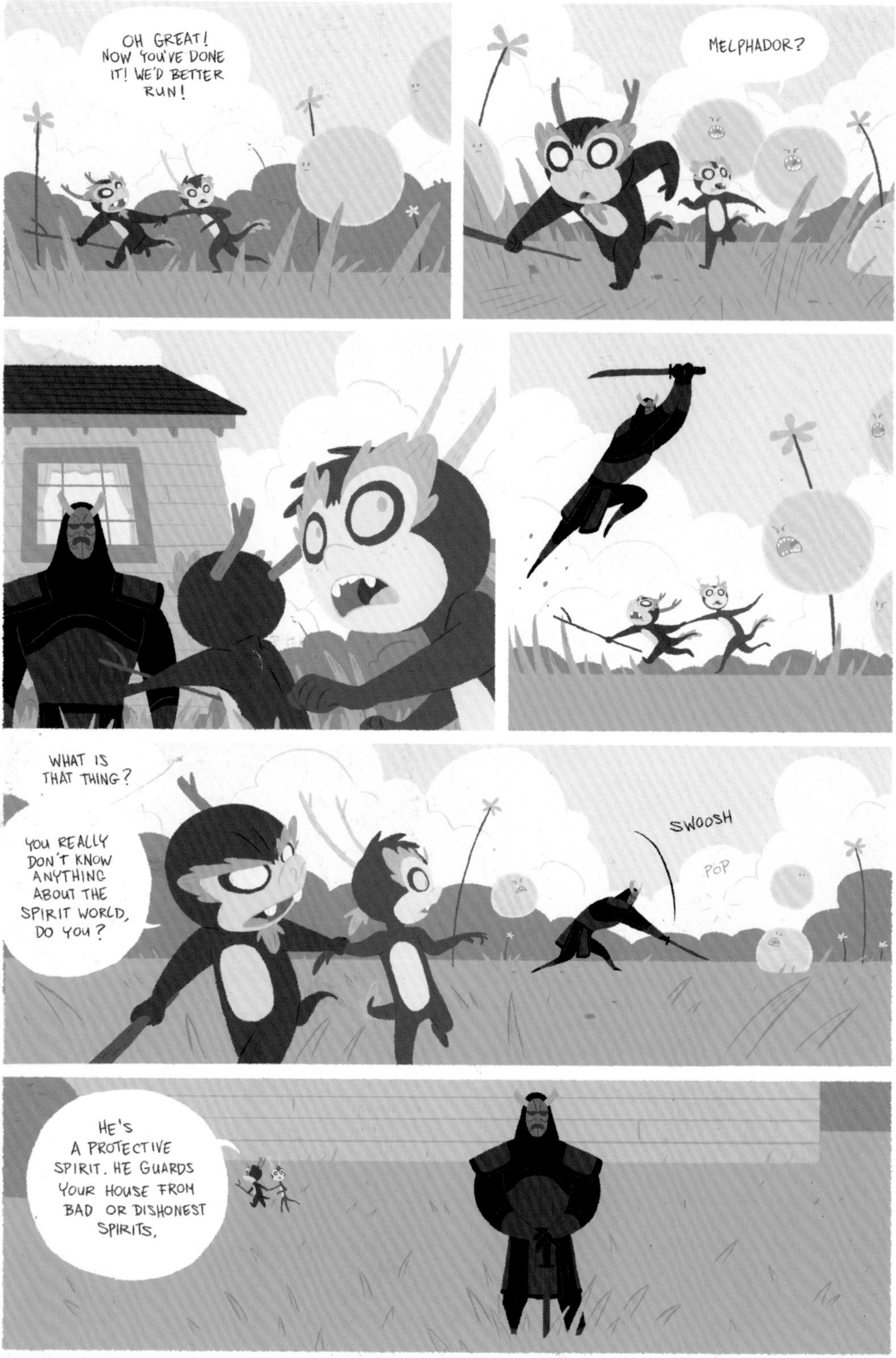
OH GREAT! NOW YOU'VE DONE IT! WE'D BETTER RUN!
MELPHADOR?
WHAT IS THAT THING?
YOU REALLY DON'T KNOW ANYTHING ABOUT THE SPIRIT WORLD, DO YOU?
SWOOSH
POP
HE'S A PROTECTIVE SPIRIT. HE GUARDS YOUR HOUSE FROM BAD OR DISHONEST SPIRITS.

SO, THIS IS HOW YOU GET IN THE HOUSE.

C'MON! TO THE THUSELA.

IS THIS ONE DANGEROUS?

OF COURSE NOT. HE WOULDN'T HAVE GOTTEN PAST THE GUARDIAN SPIRIT IF HE WAS.

OH...

PAT PAT

THEN, HOW DID YOU GET PAST THE GUARDIAN SPIRIT?

HA-HA! VERY FUNNY, HUMAN.

OK. WE'RE HERE. THE THUSELA IS PAST THE PILLARS OF DOOM!

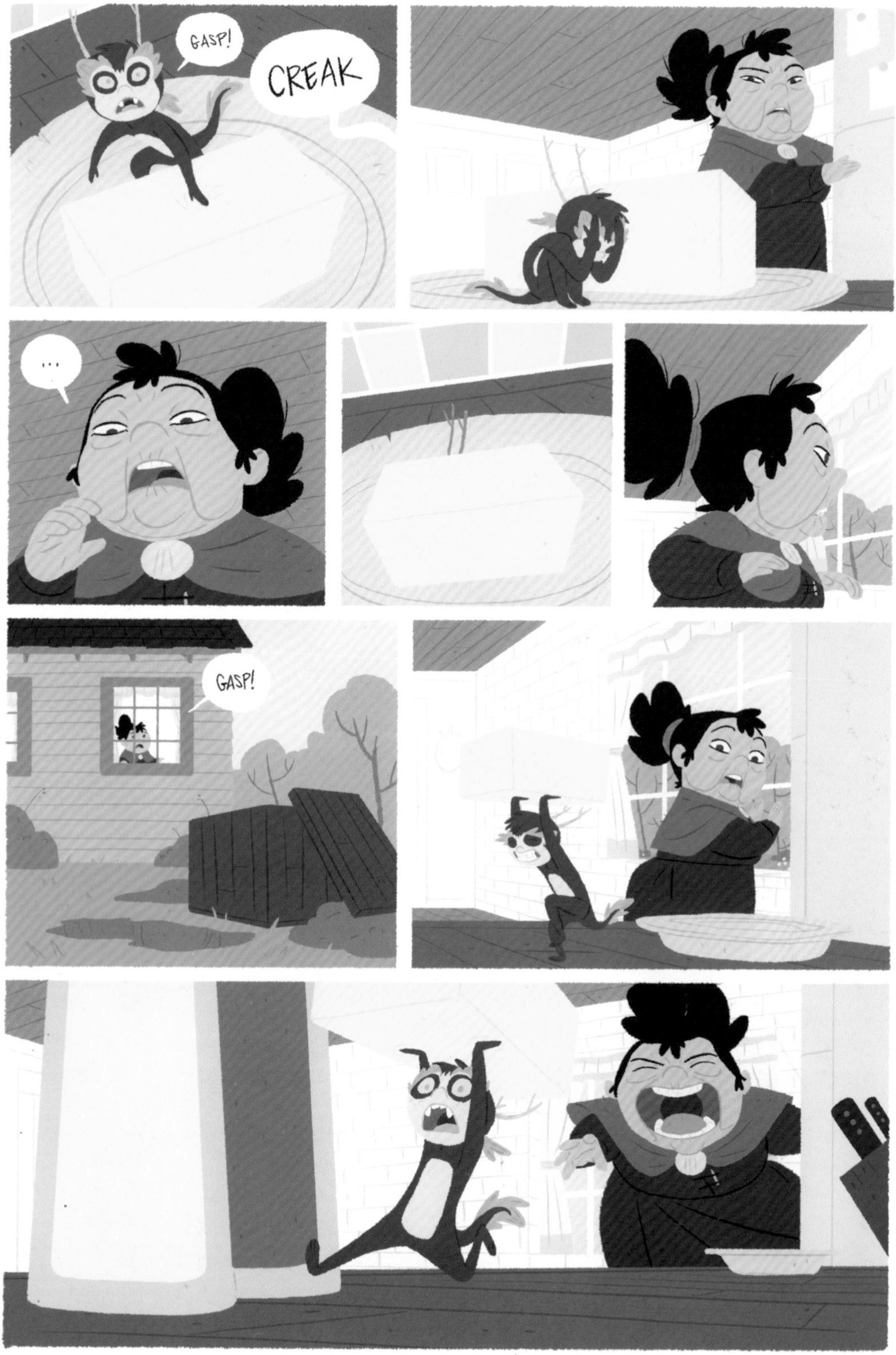
GASP!
CREAK
...
GASP!

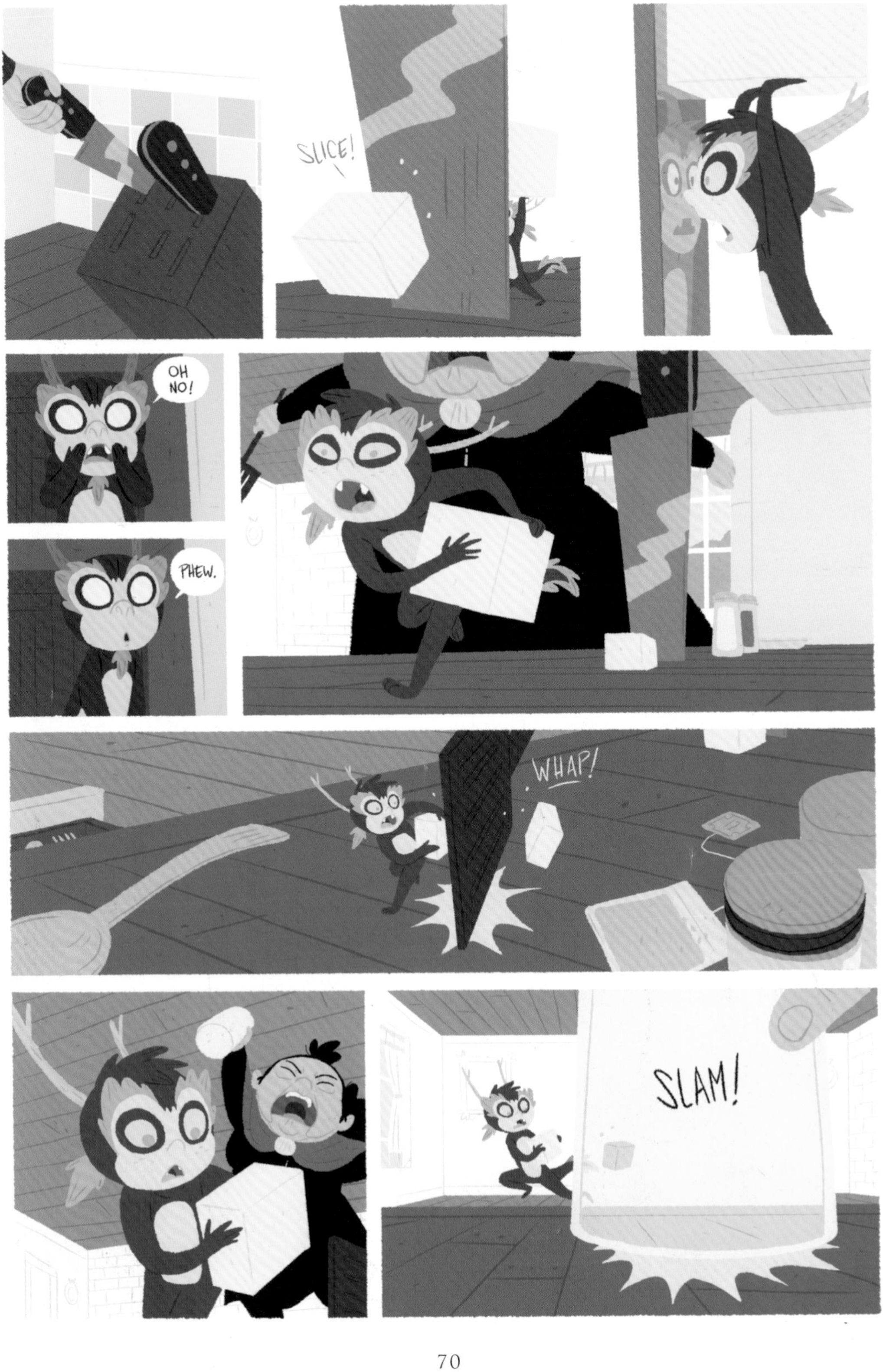
SLICE!
OH NO!
PHEW.
WHAP!
SLAM!

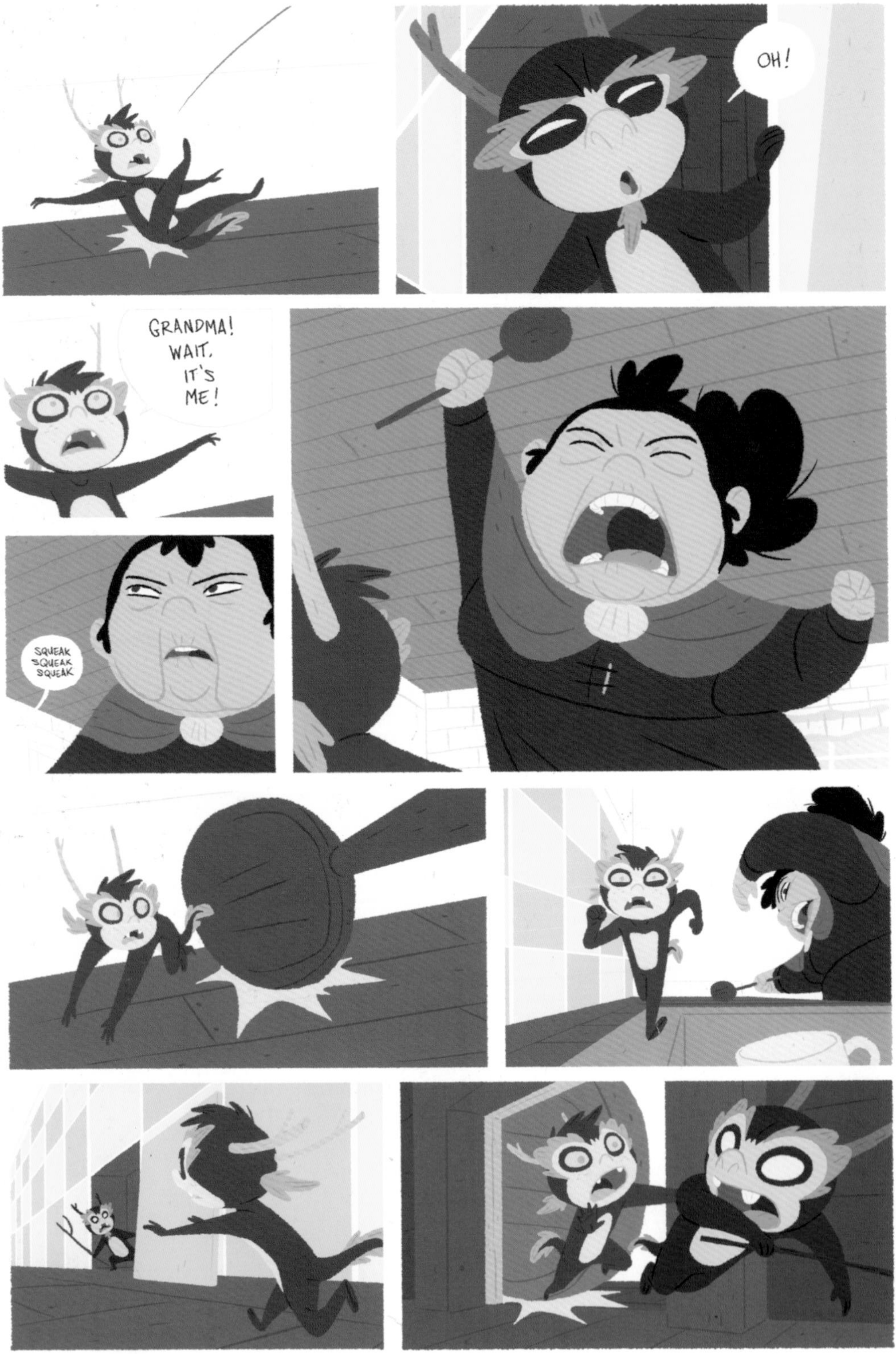
OH!
GRANDMA! WAIT. IT'S ME!
SQUEAK SQUEAK SQUEAK

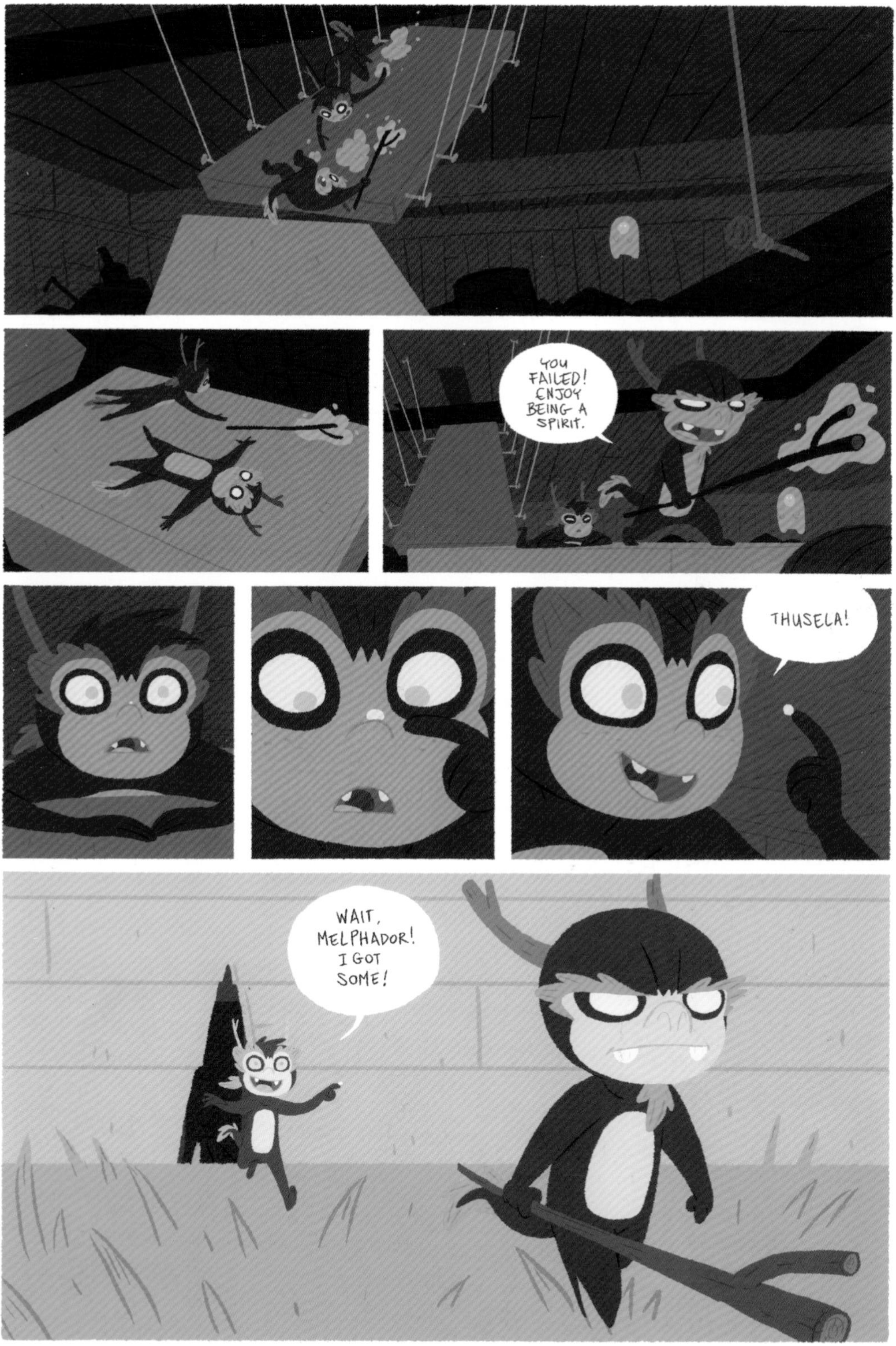
YOU FAILED! ENJOY BEING A SPIRIT.
THUSELA!
WAIT, MELPHADOR! I GOT SOME!

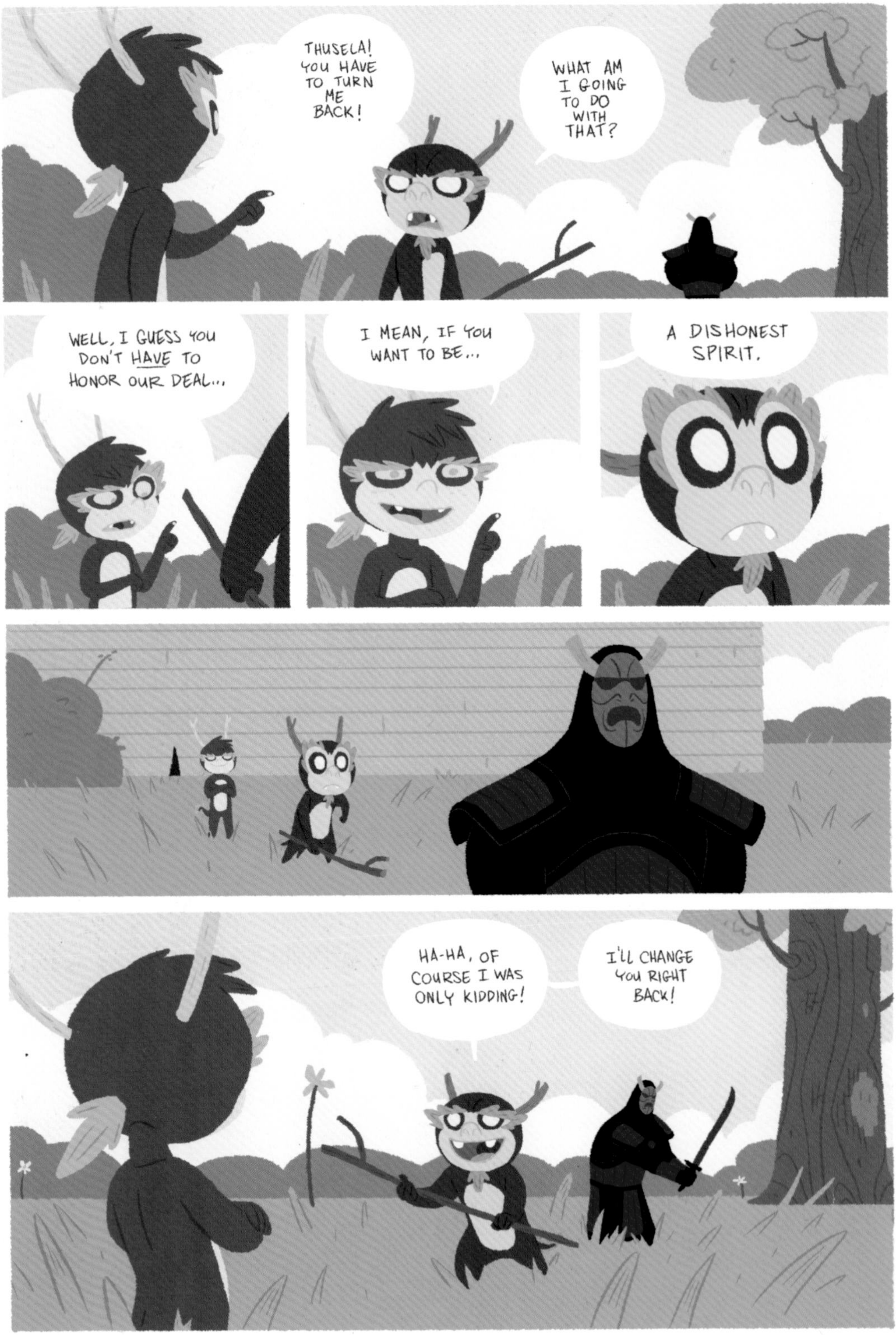
THUSELA! YOU HAVE TO TURN ME BACK!
WHAT AM I GOING TO DO WITH THAT?
WELL, I GUESS YOU DON'T HAVE TO HONOR OUR DEAL...
I MEAN, IF YOU WANT TO BE...
A DISHONEST SPIRIT.
HA-HA, OF COURSE I WAS ONLY KIDDING!
I'LL CHANGE YOU RIGHT BACK!

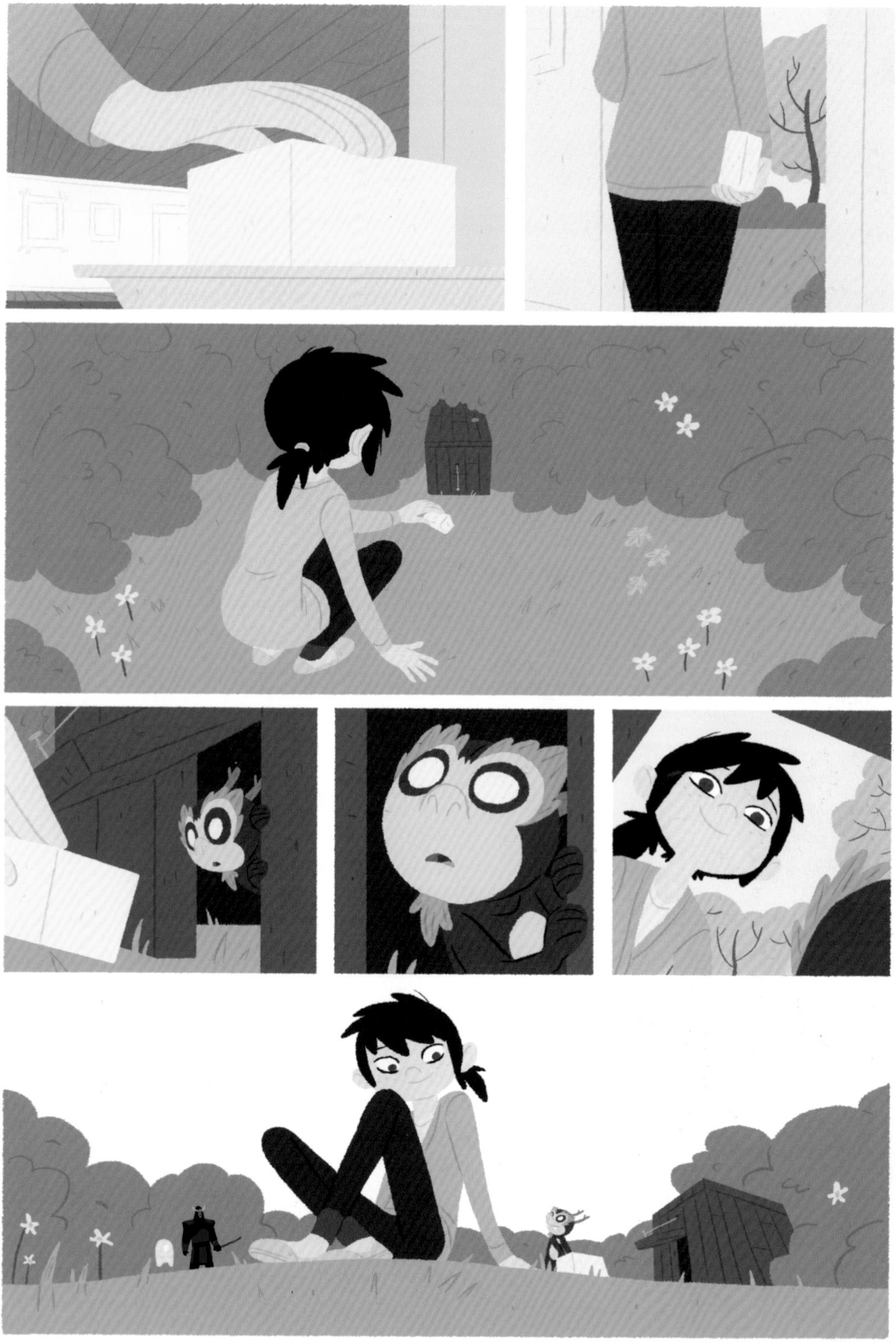

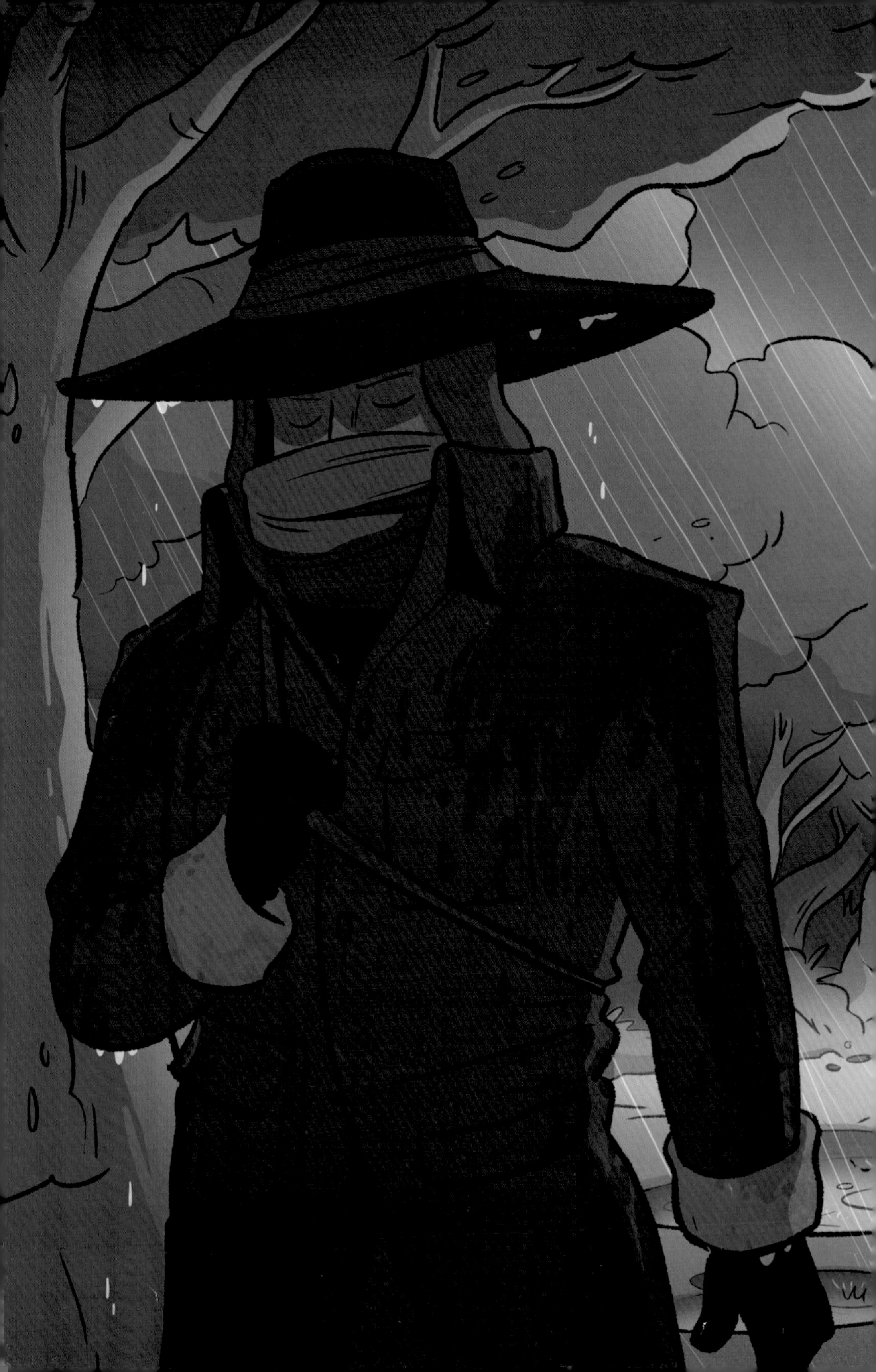

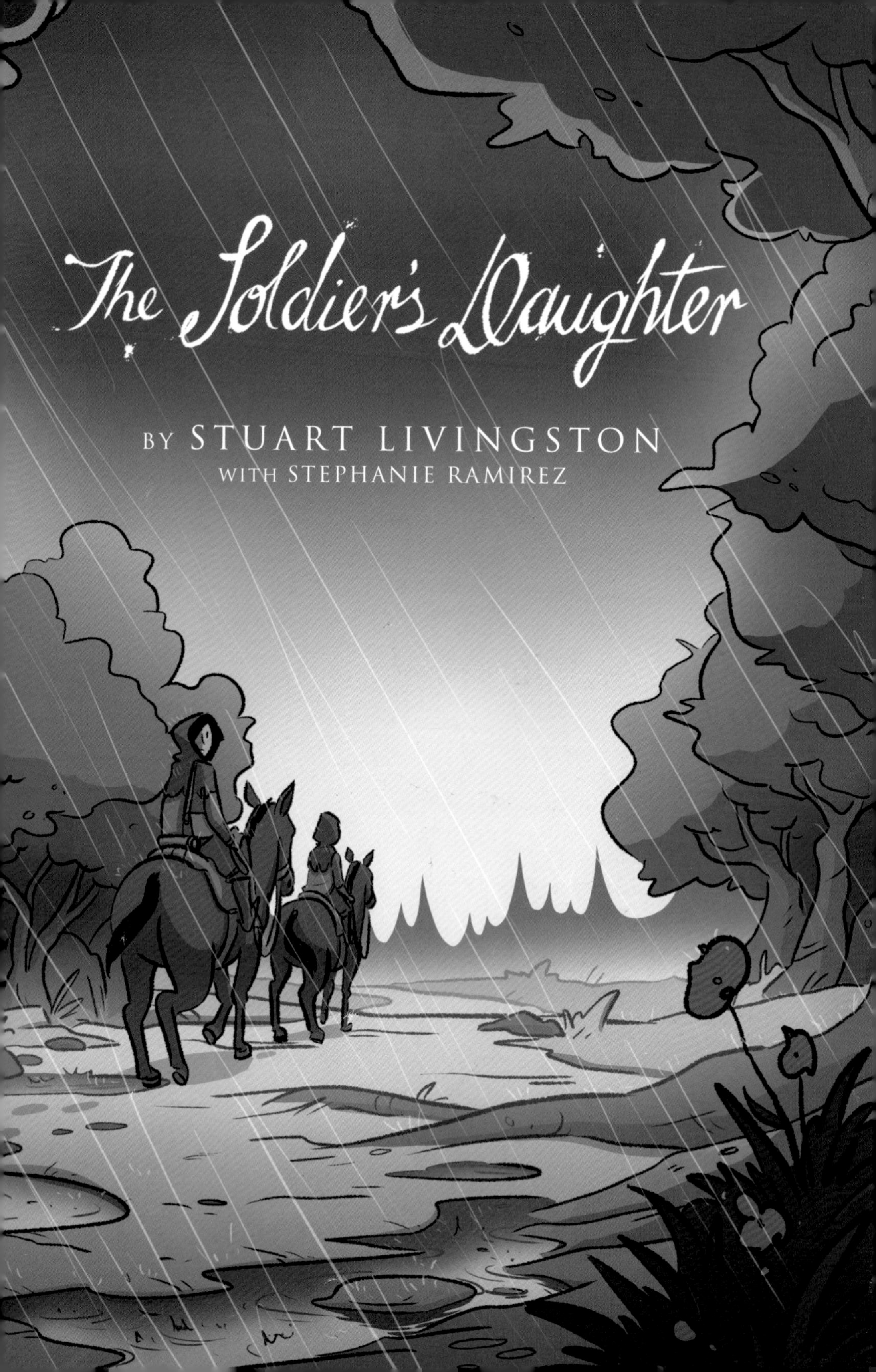
The Soldier's Daughter
BY STUART LIVINGSTON
WITH STEPHANIE RAMIREZ

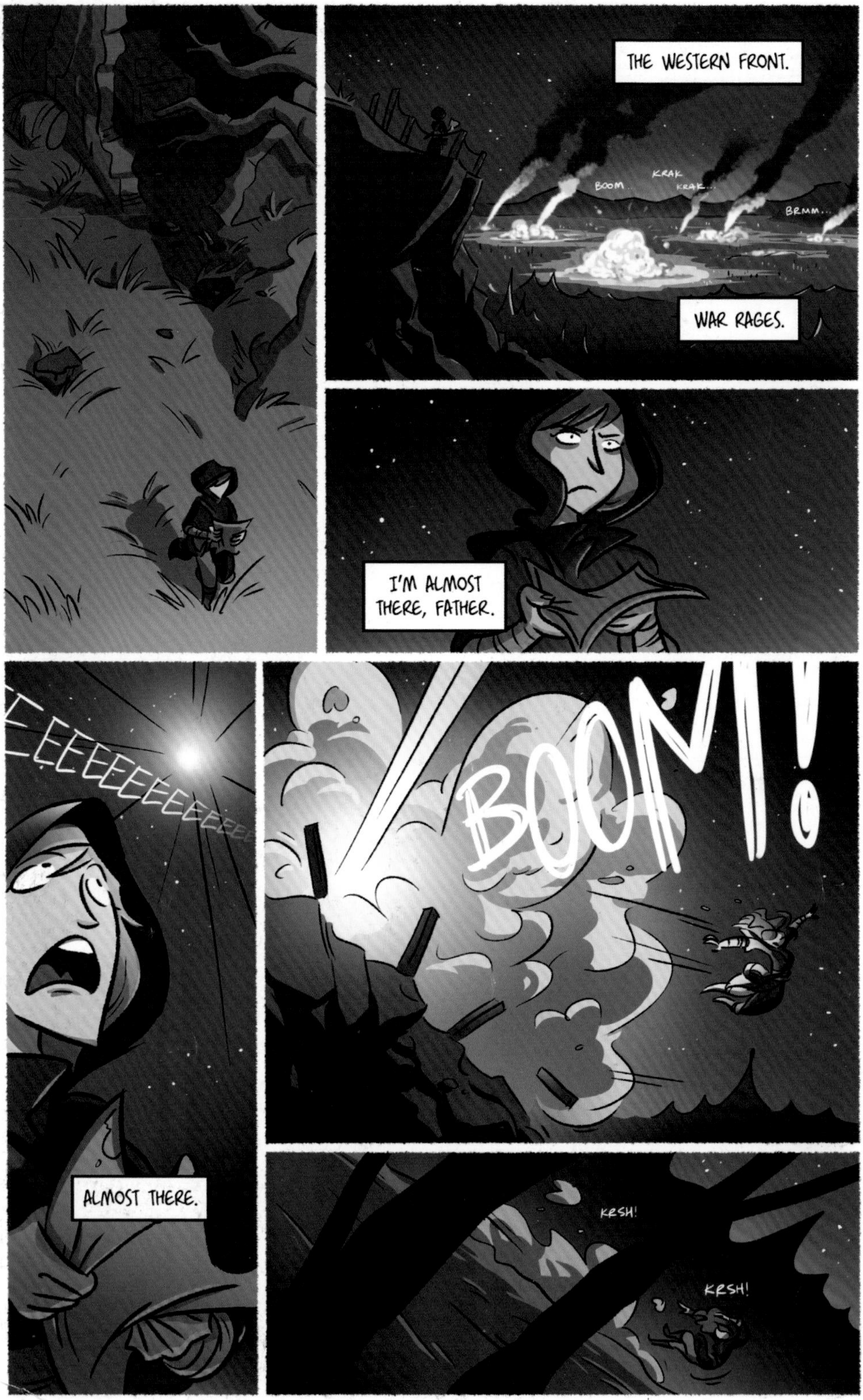
THE WESTERN FRONT.
BOOM...
KRAK
KRAK...
BRMM...
WAR RAGES.
I'M ALMOST THERE, FATHER.
BOOM!
ALMOST THERE.
KRSH!
KRSH!

83

WAR IS A DARK POWER, CLARA.

MANY WHO RIDE IN BATTLE WILL FIND THIS POWER—MANY MORE WILL BE CONSUMED BY IT. NOT EVERYONE HAS THE STRENGTH TO RESIST.

CAPTAIN VAAL, FOR ONE...

WH—WHAT DID YOU SAY?

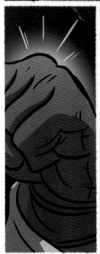

CAN I SAVE THIS ONE, TOO?

FWOOM!

AND YOUR FATHER...

SHK!

WHO ARE YOU? A SPY?!

NO...A MESSENGER.

WITH AN URGENT DELIVERY.

WHAT...

WHAT IS THIS?

85

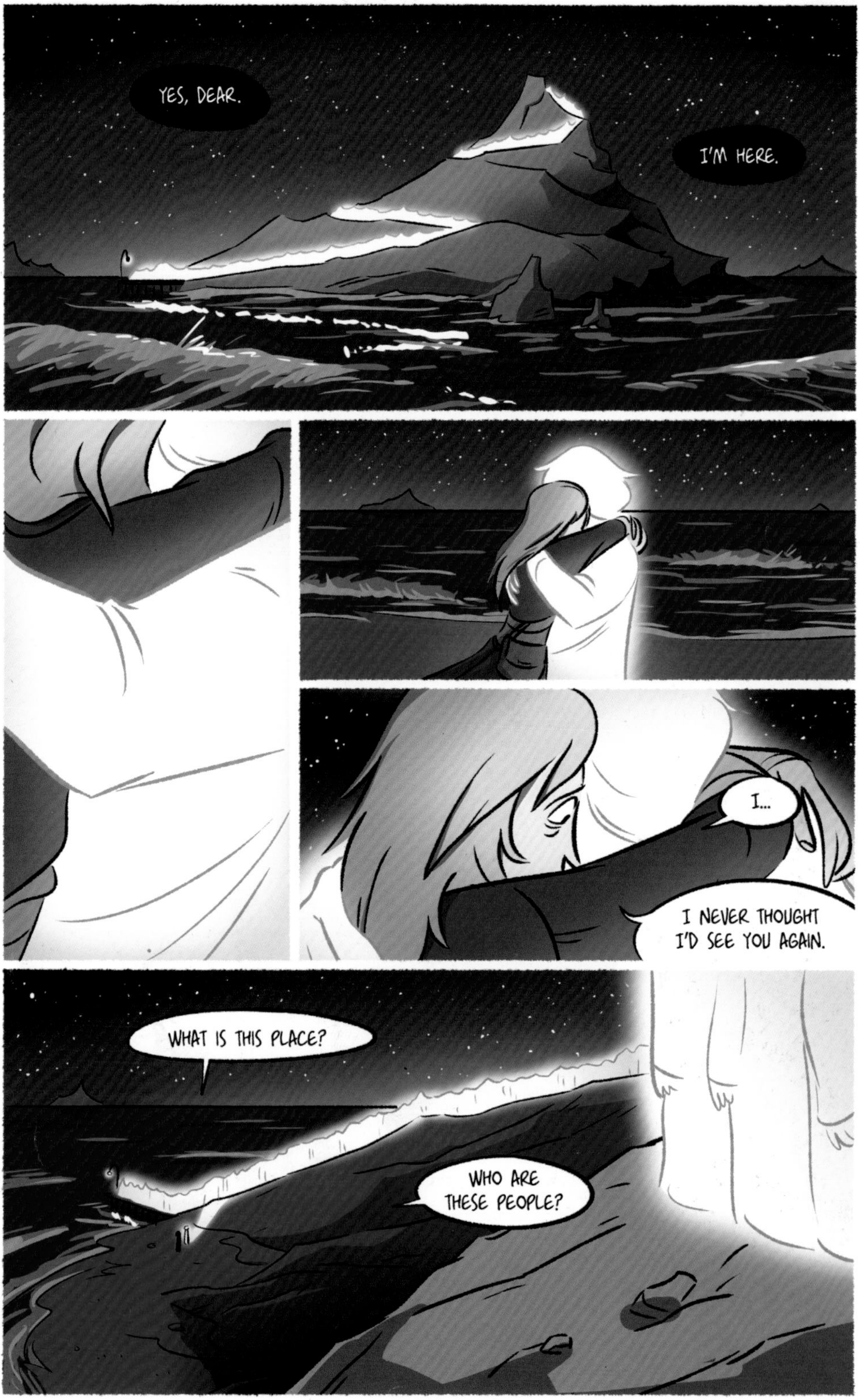
YES, DEAR.
I'M HERE.
I...
I NEVER THOUGHT I'D SEE YOU AGAIN.
WHAT IS THIS PLACE?
WHO ARE THESE PEOPLE?

WHY ARE WE HERE, FATHER?

I'M AFRAID THIS IS MY DOING.

I KNOW WHAT YOU INTEND TO DO. AND I CAN'T LET THAT HAPPEN.

CLARA.

DON'T LET YOUR ANGER DESTROY YOU...AS I DID.

IN THE THICK OF BATTLE, AS MY SWORD CLANGED AND STRUCK HOME...

A GREAT DARKNESS GREW WITHIN ME.

I TRIED TO FIGHT IT, WITH THOUGHTS OF YOU...

AND JACK...

BUT IT WAS TOO LATE.

88

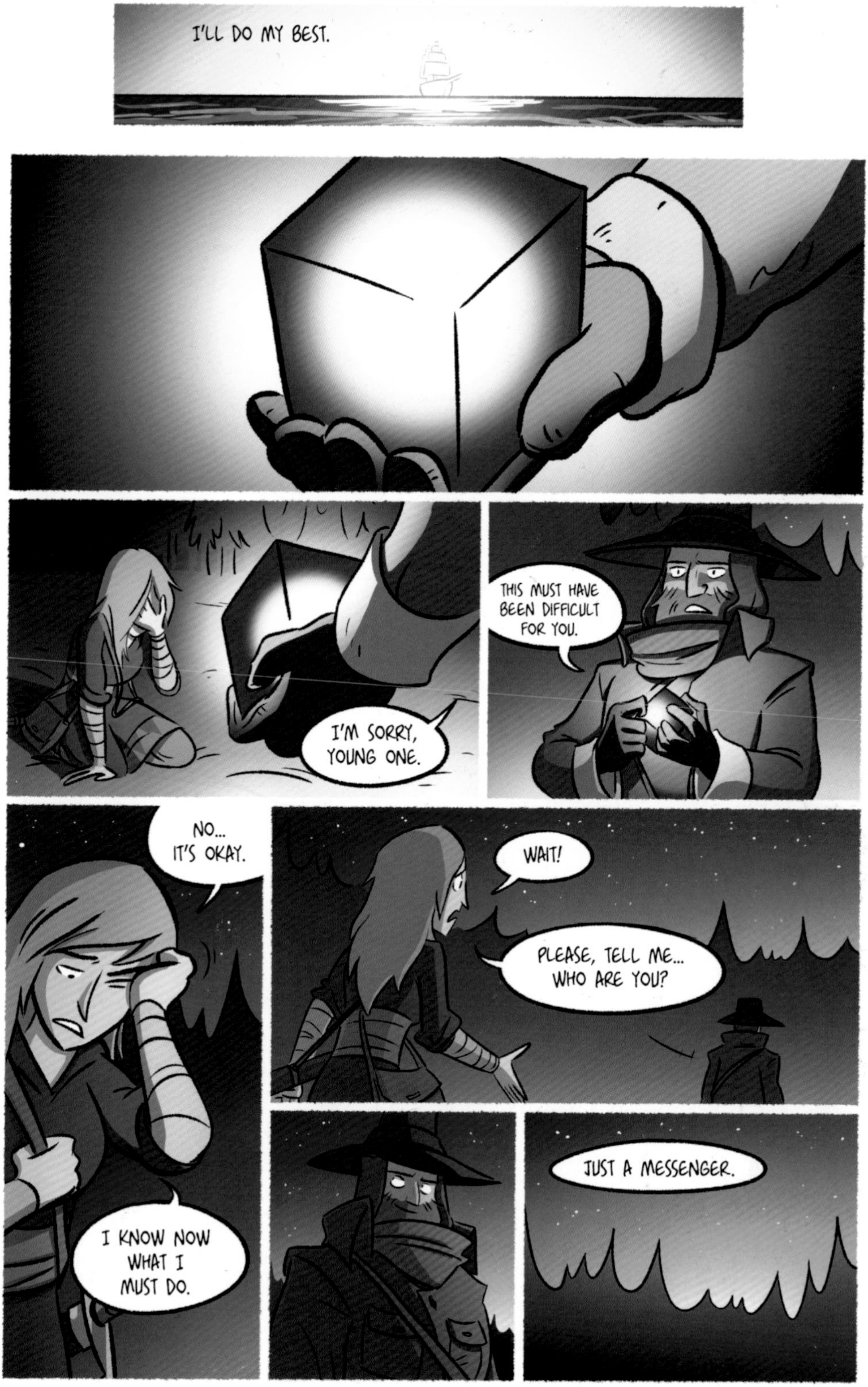
I'LL DO MY BEST.
I'M SORRY, YOUNG ONE.
THIS MUST HAVE BEEN DIFFICULT FOR YOU.
NO... IT'S OKAY.
I KNOW NOW WHAT I MUST DO.
WAIT!
PLEASE, TELL ME... WHO ARE YOU?
JUST A MESSENGER.

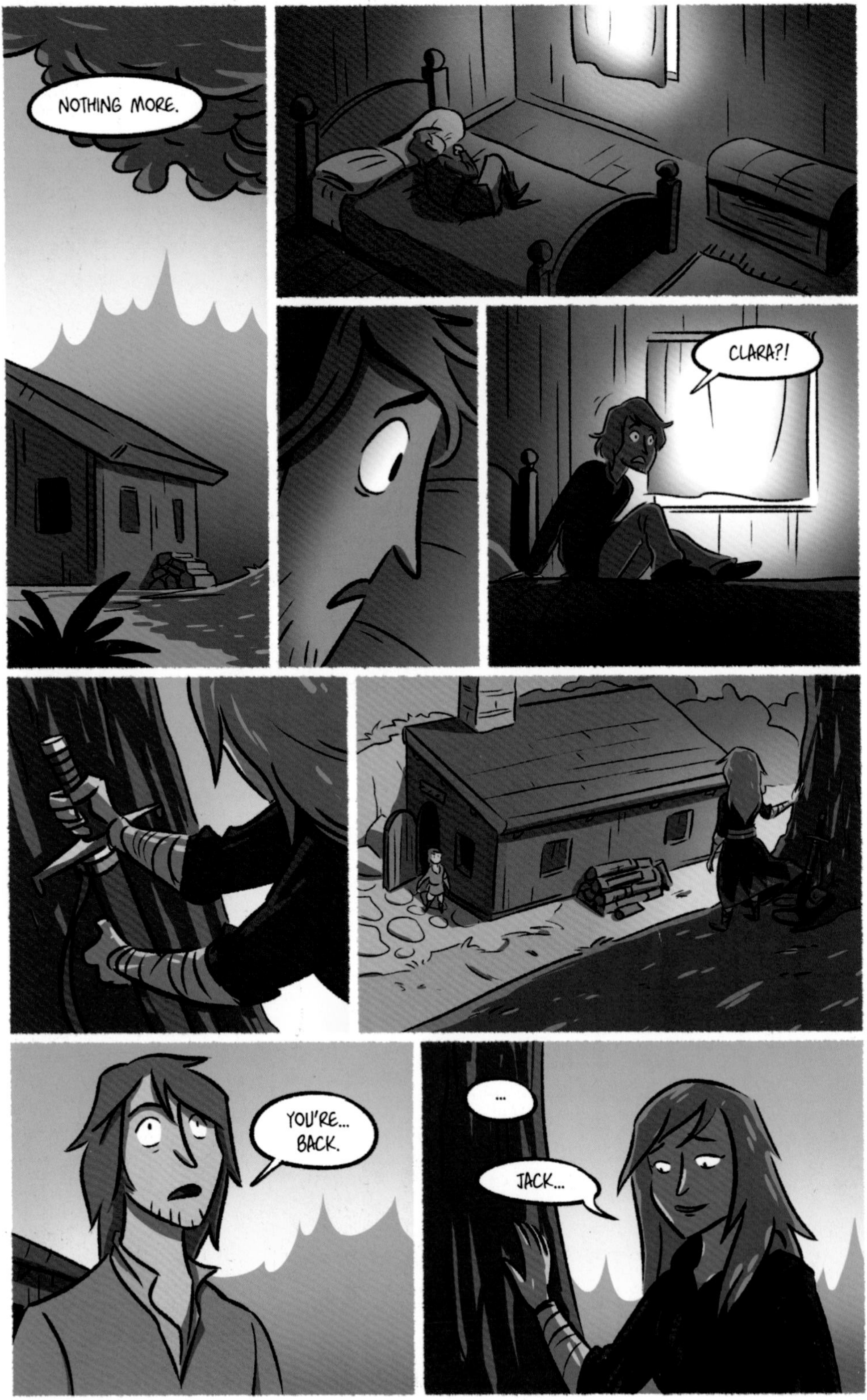
NOTHING MORE.
CLARA?!
YOU'RE... BACK.
...
JACK...

END.

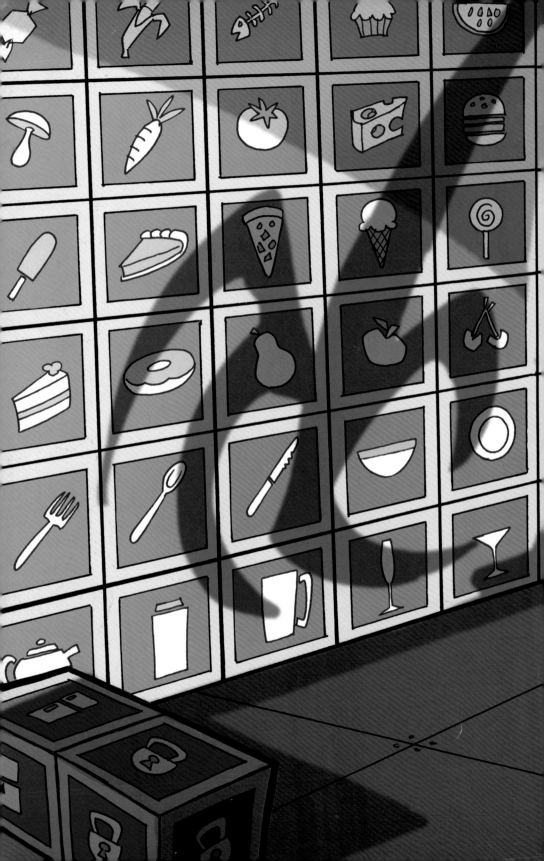

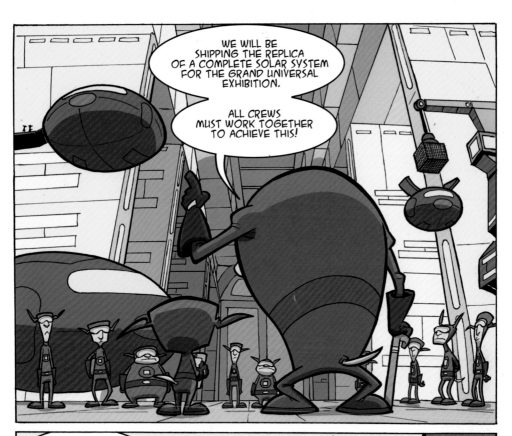

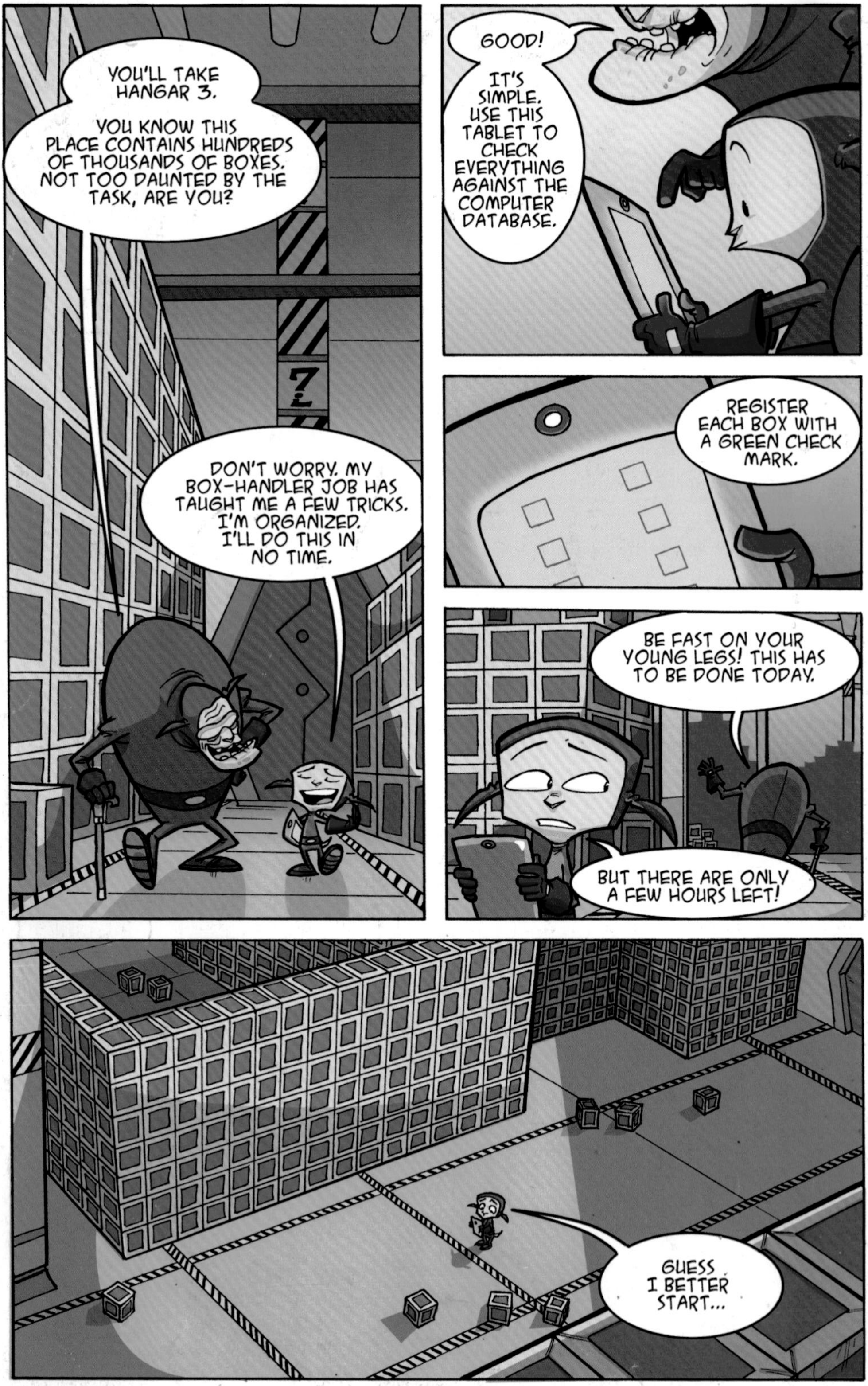
YOU'LL TAKE HANGAR 3.
YOU KNOW THIS PLACE CONTAINS HUNDREDS OF THOUSANDS OF BOXES. NOT TOO DAUNTED BY THE TASK, ARE YOU?
DON'T WORRY. MY BOX-HANDLER JOB HAS TAUGHT ME A FEW TRICKS. I'M ORGANIZED. I'LL DO THIS IN NO TIME.
GOOD!
IT'S SIMPLE. USE THIS TABLET TO CHECK EVERYTHING AGAINST THE COMPUTER DATABASE.
REGISTER EACH BOX WITH A GREEN CHECK MARK.
BE FAST ON YOUR YOUNG LEGS! THIS HAS TO BE DONE TODAY.
BUT THERE ARE ONLY A FEW HOURS LEFT!
GUESS I BETTER START...

KER-FLASH!

KERFLASH!

KER-FLASH!

KER-FLASH!

KER-FLASH!

KERFLASH!

KER-FLASH!

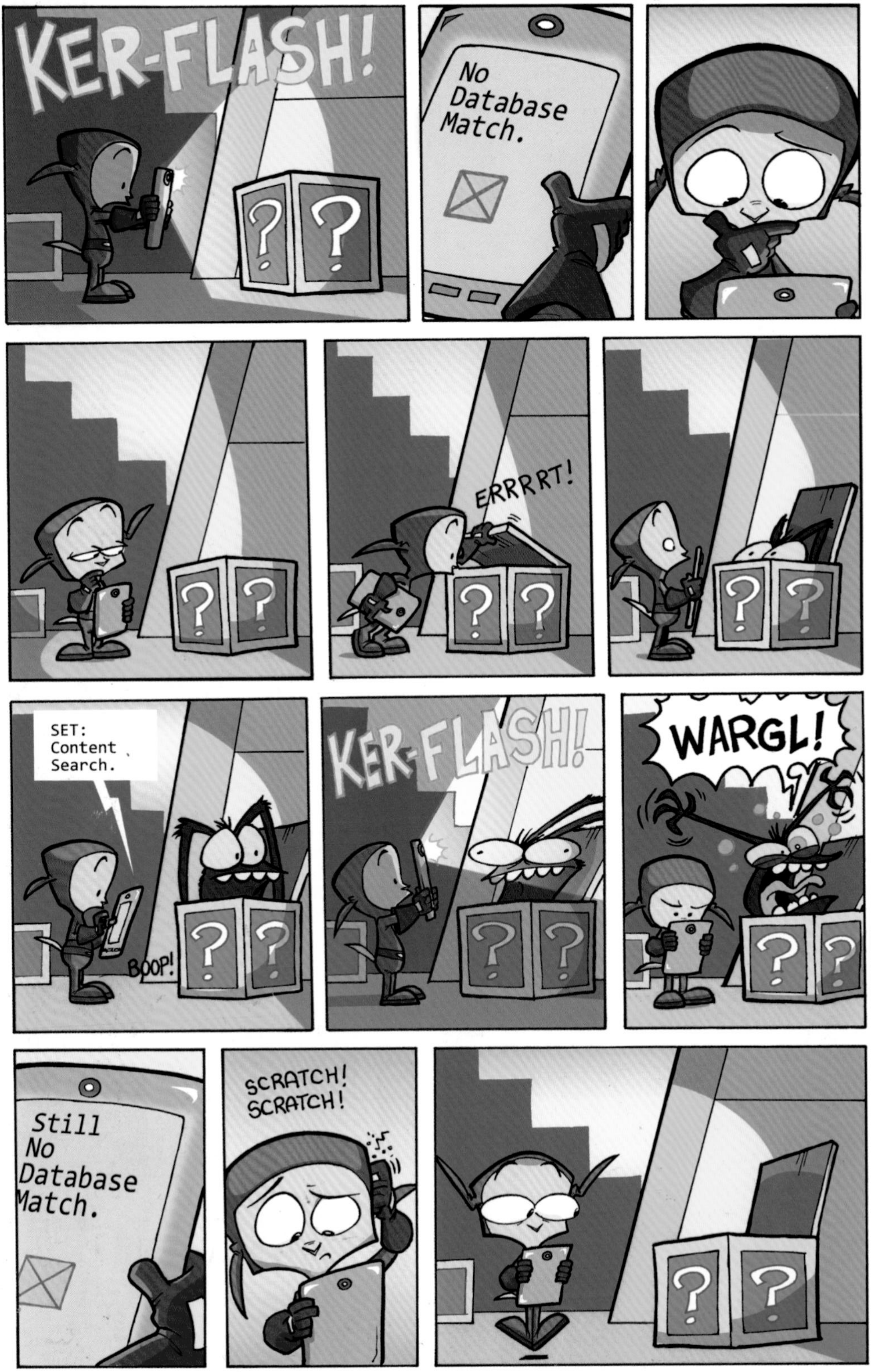
KER-FLASH!
No Database Match.
SET: Content Search.
BOOP!
ERRRRT!
KER-FLASH!
WARGL!
Still No Database Match.
SCRATCH! SCRATCH!

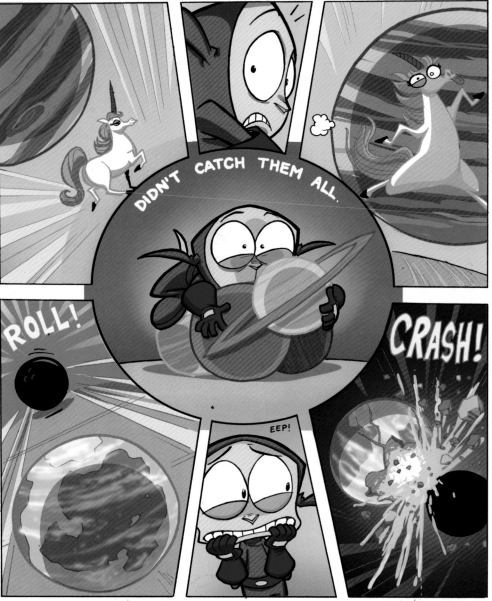

NAGL?

YOU! GET OVER—

DEET?

JUST CHECKING IN.

IS ALL GOING WELL?

OHYESGRAMPAABSOLUTELY EVERYTHINGISGOINGSMOOTHLY TIPTOPSHAPENOWORRIES!!

GOOD! I'LL DROP BY FOR A SHORT VISIT LATER.

UH-OH.

I HAVE TO QUICKLY CLEAN ALL THIS

BUT I BETTER CAPTURE THAT THING FIRST OR IT WILL KEEP MESSING EVERYTHING UP!

HMMM...

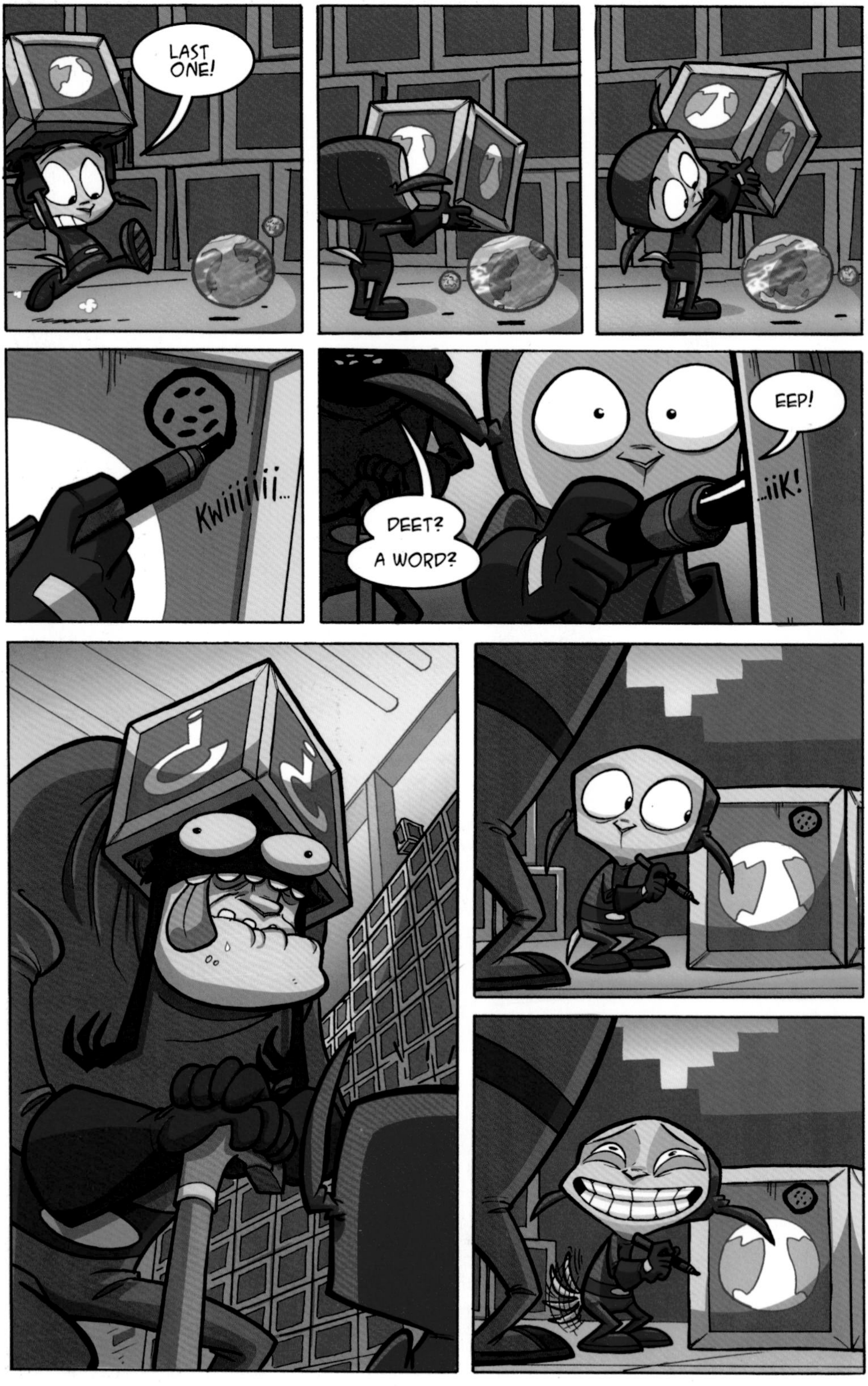
LAST ONE!
KWIIIIIII...
DEET? A WORD?
EEP!
...IIK!

POOR GRAMPA. I'VE RUINED HIS DAY.

I BETTER ASK THESE GUYS WHERE THIS BOX GOES. I DON'T WANT TO MESS UP AGAIN...

HA HA HA

DON'T YOU THINK USING THE WHATZIT WAS A BIT CRUEL FOR A PRANK?

NAH, THE KID DESERVED IT!

EASY FOR YOU TO SAY! I HAVE TO DEAL WITH ALL THOSE BROKEN BOXES.

HE THOUGHT HE COULD JUMP RANK EASY WITH HELP FROM HIS GRAMPA...

BUT HIS JUMP WAS MORE LIKE A TUMBLE!

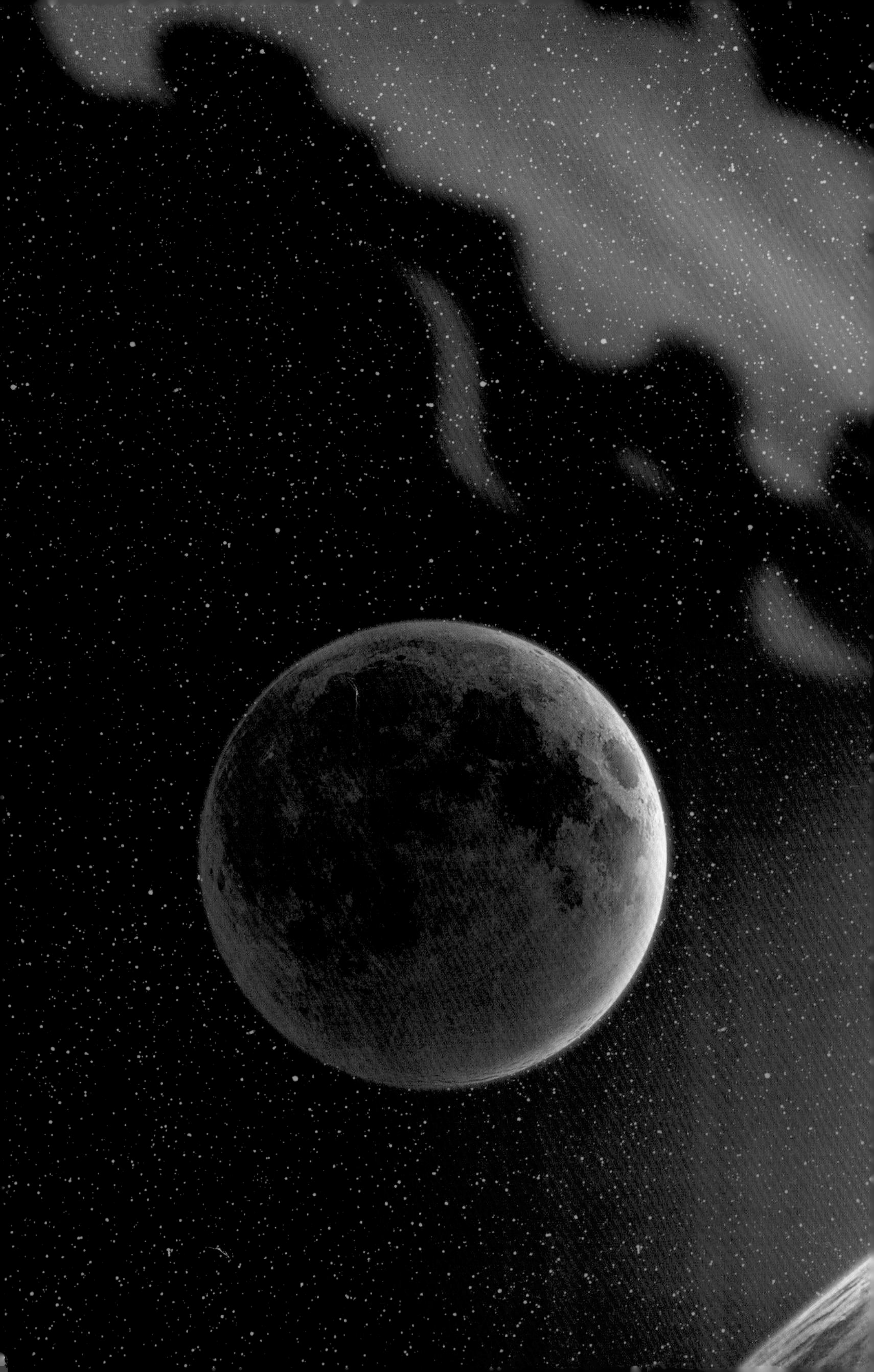

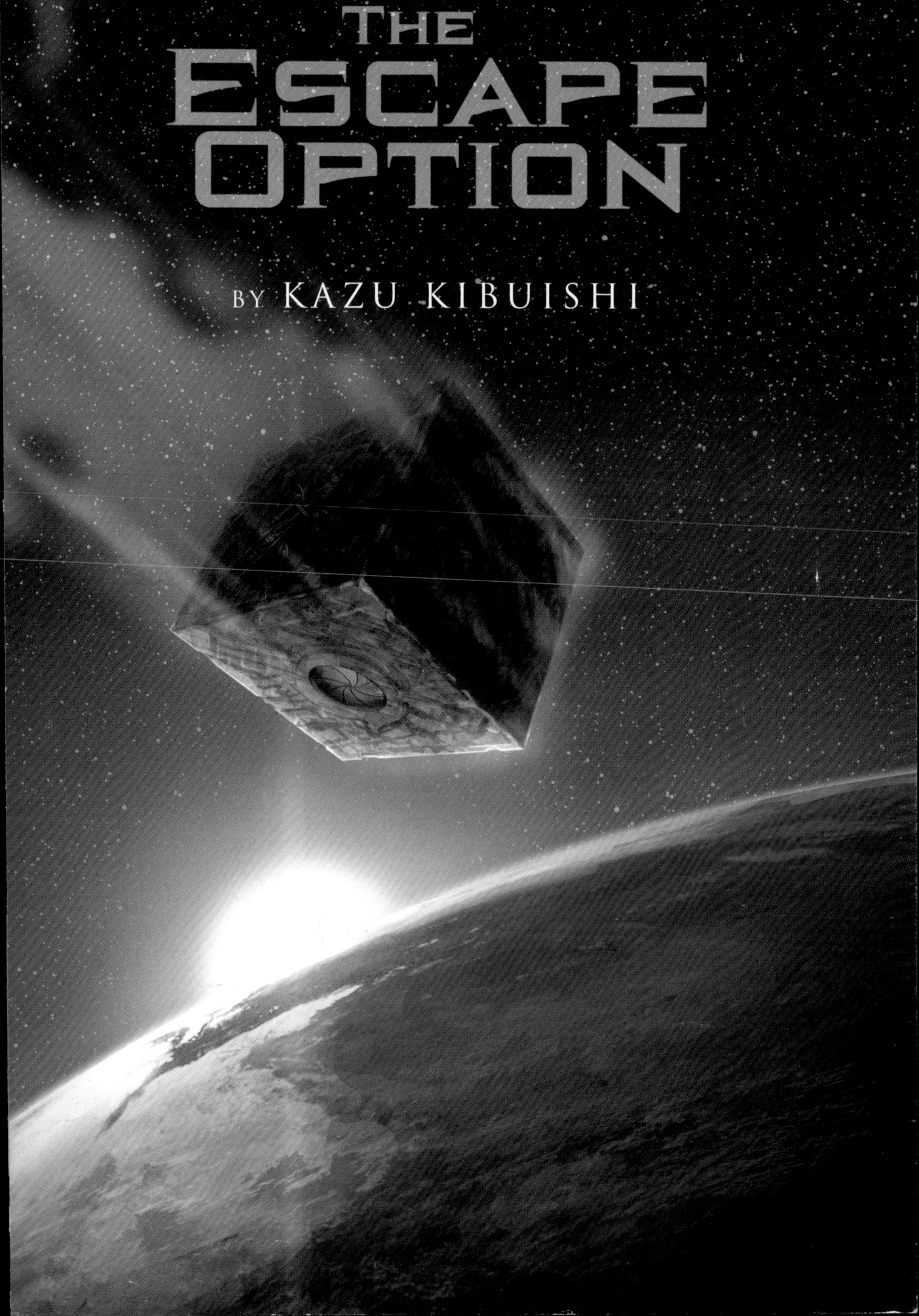
THE ESCAPE OPTION
BY KAZU KIBUISHI

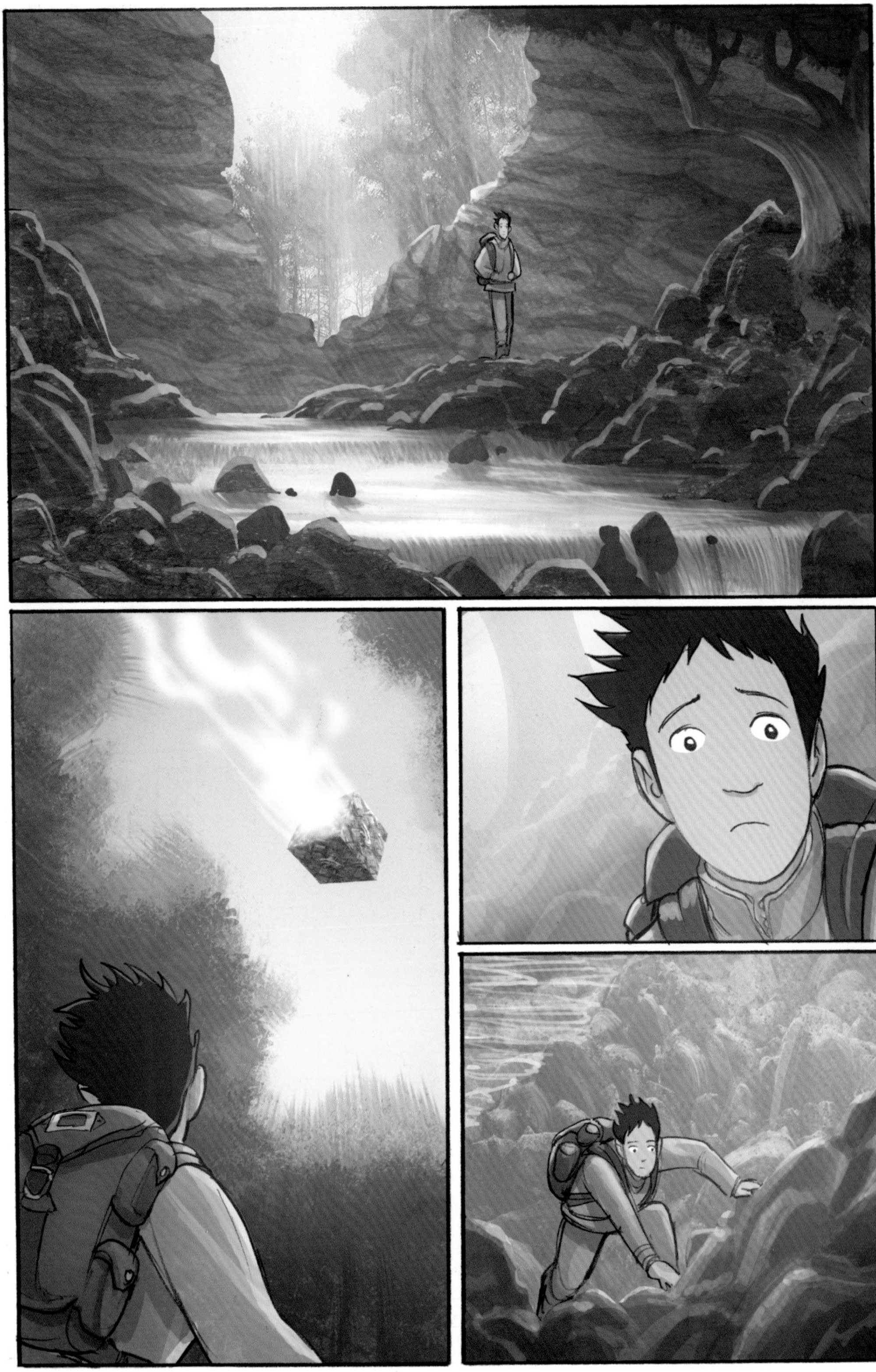

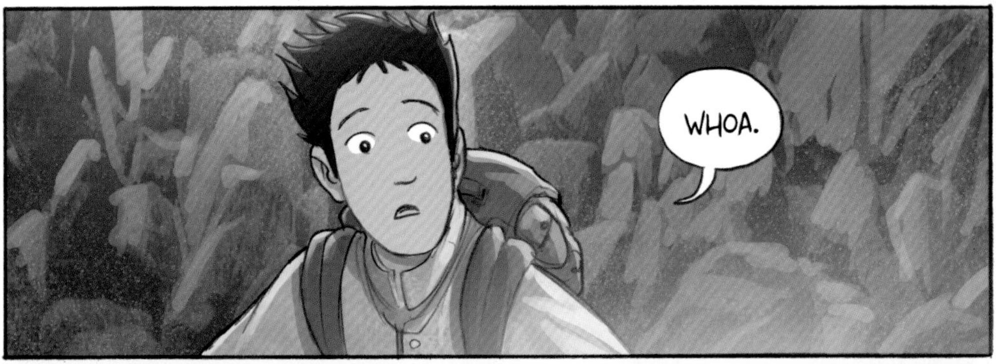
WHOA.

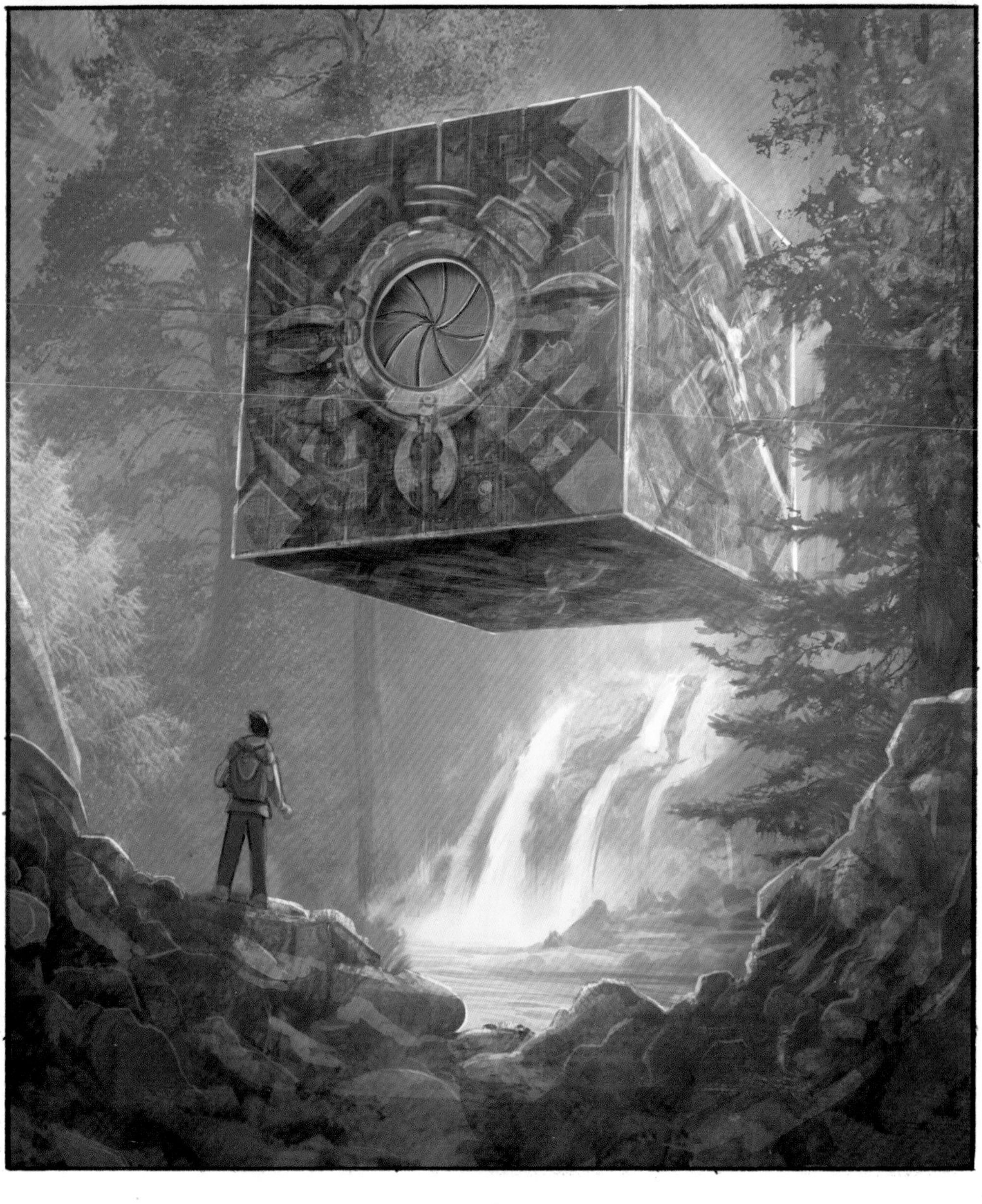

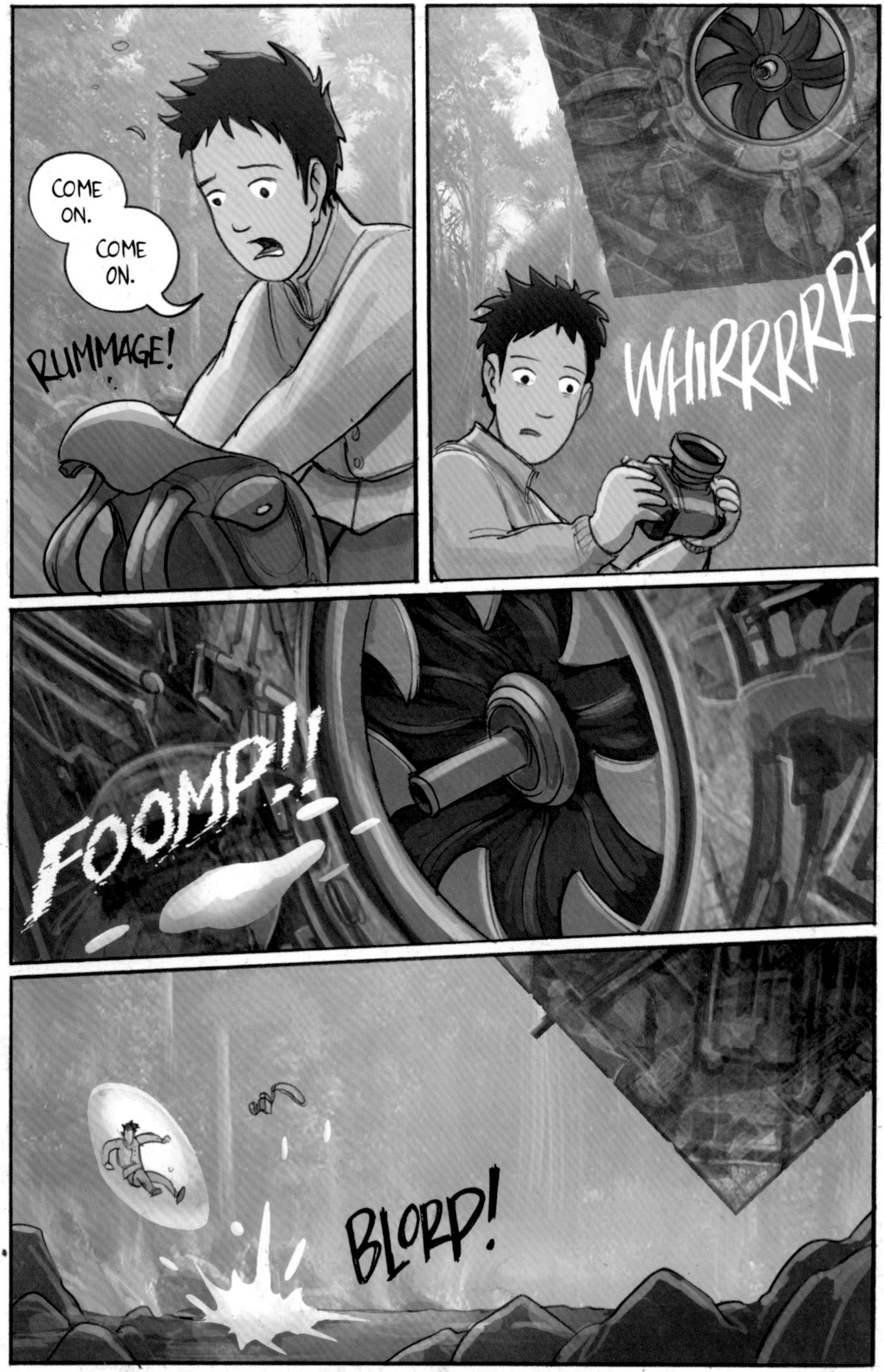
COME ON.
COME ON.
RUMMAGE!
WHIRRRRRR
FOOMP!!
BLORD!

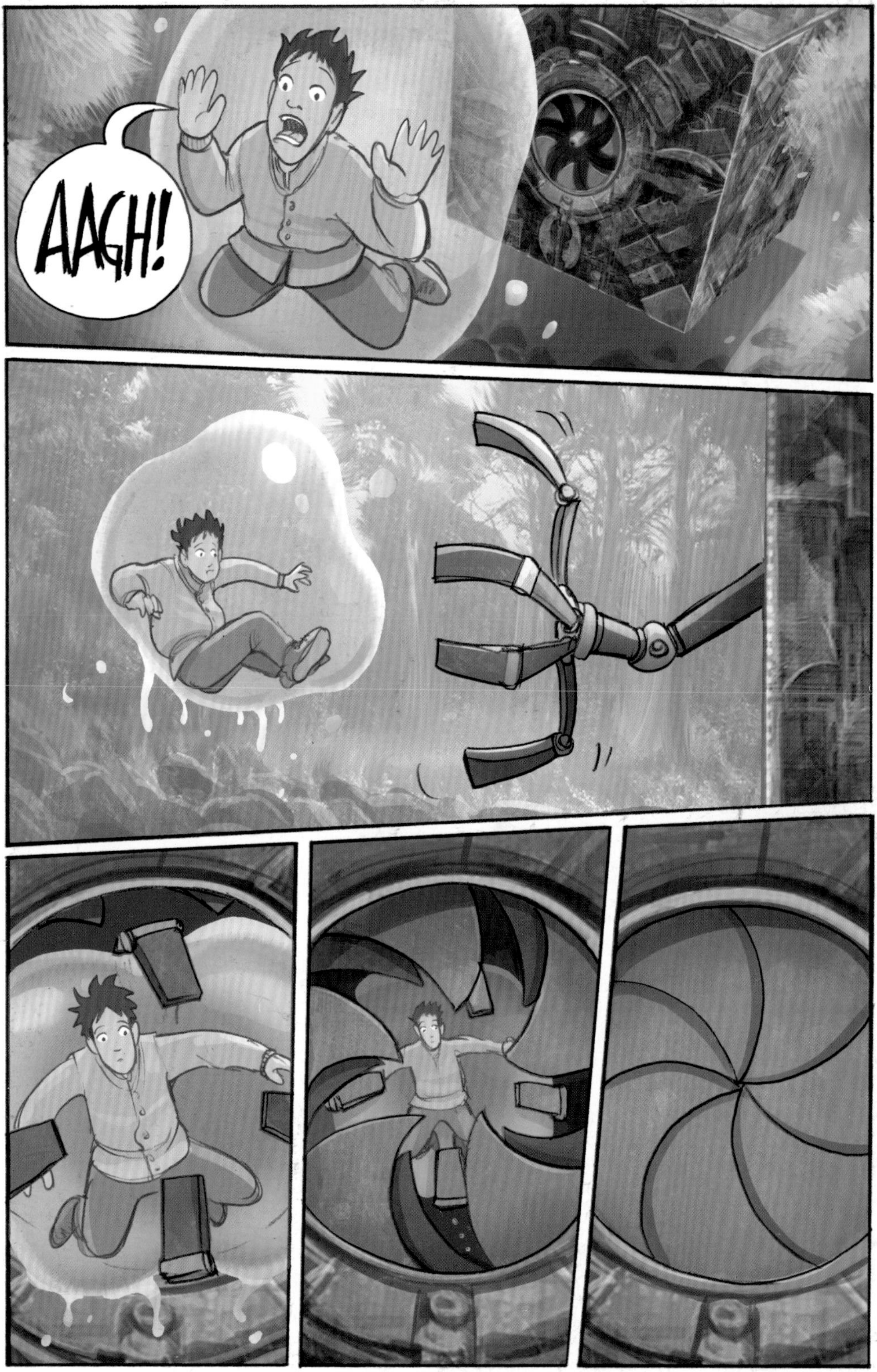
AAGH!

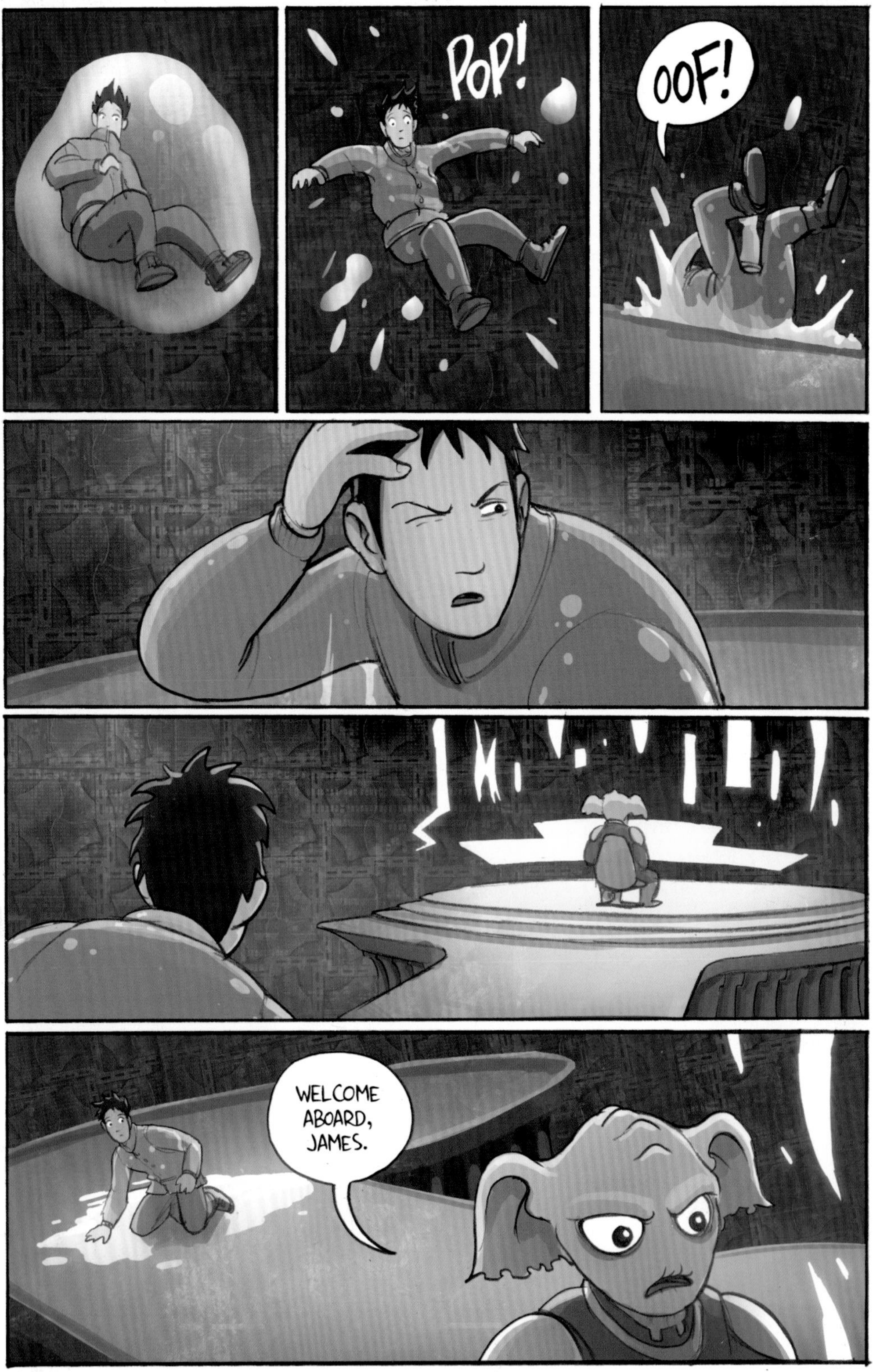
POP!
OOF!
WELCOME ABOARD, JAMES.

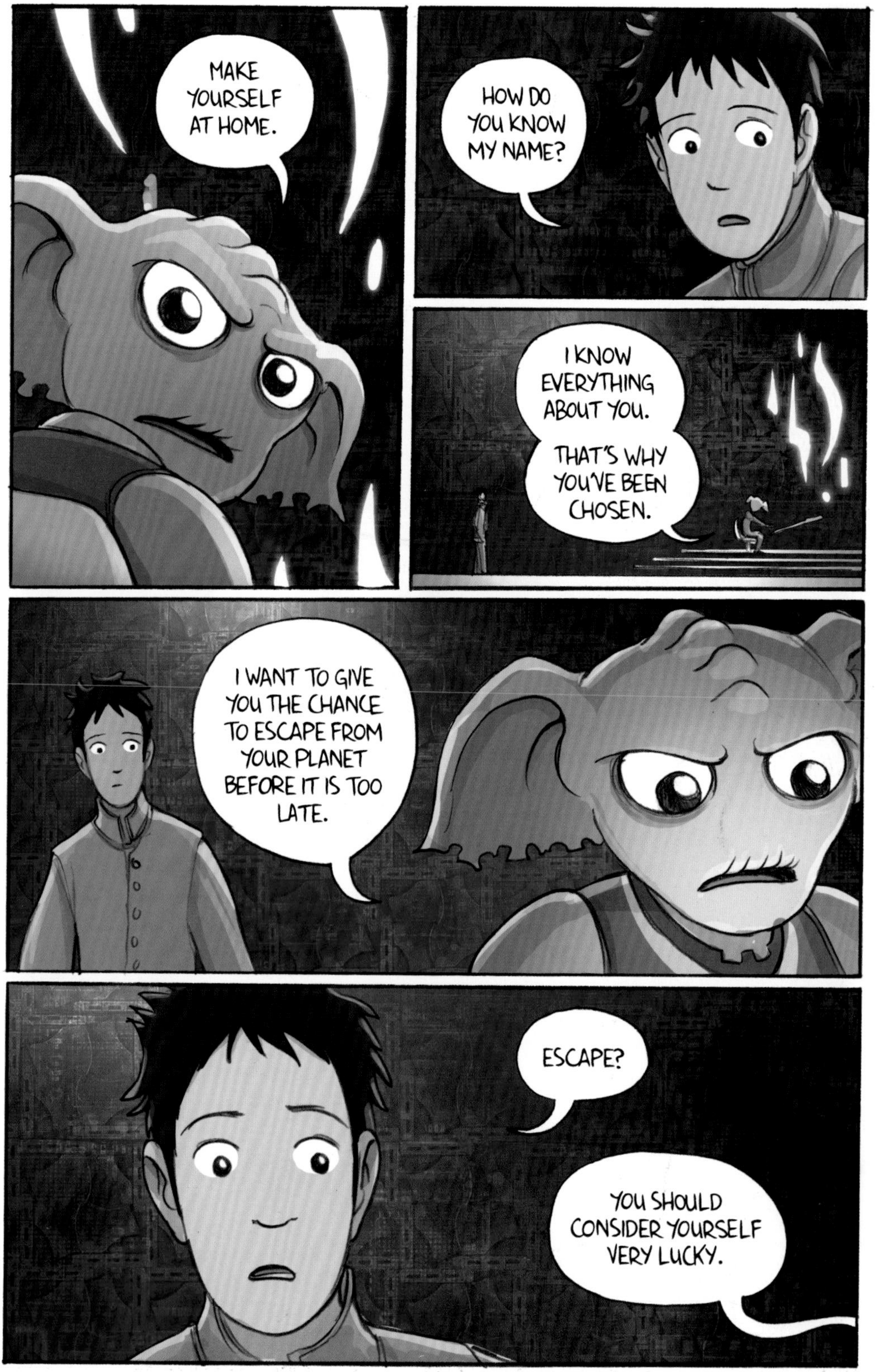
MAKE YOURSELF AT HOME.
HOW DO YOU KNOW MY NAME?
I KNOW EVERYTHING ABOUT YOU.
THAT'S WHY YOU'VE BEEN CHOSEN.
I WANT TO GIVE YOU THE CHANCE TO ESCAPE FROM YOUR PLANET BEFORE IT IS TOO LATE.
ESCAPE?
YOU SHOULD CONSIDER YOURSELF VERY LUCKY.

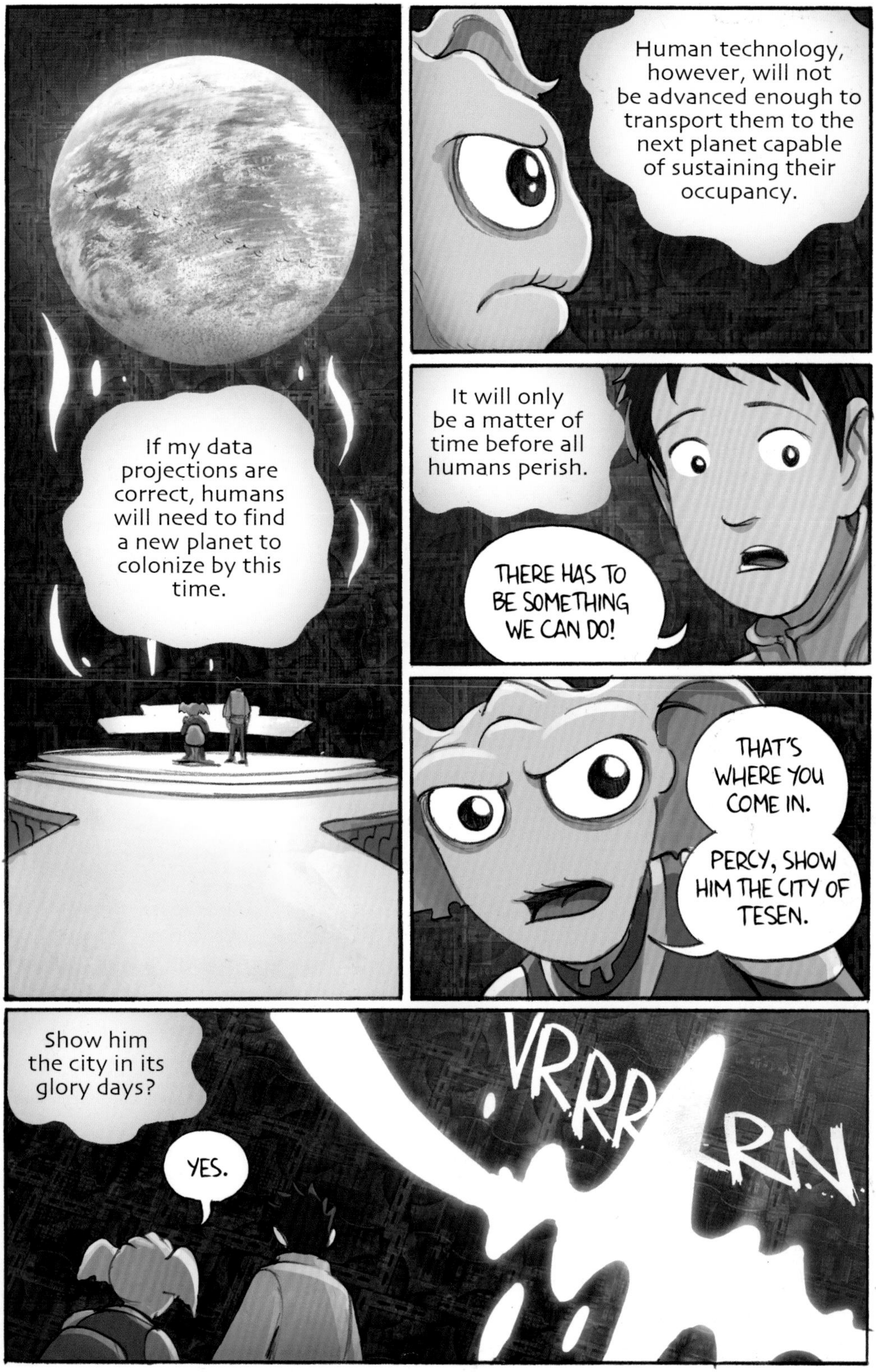

If my data projections are correct, humans will need to find a new planet to colonize by this time.
Human technology, however, will not be advanced enough to transport them to the next planet capable of sustaining their occupancy.
It will only be a matter of time before all humans perish.
THERE HAS TO BE SOMETHING WE CAN DO!
THAT'S WHERE YOU COME IN.
PERCY, SHOW HIM THE CITY OF TESEN.
Show him the city in its glory days?
YES.
VRRRRRN

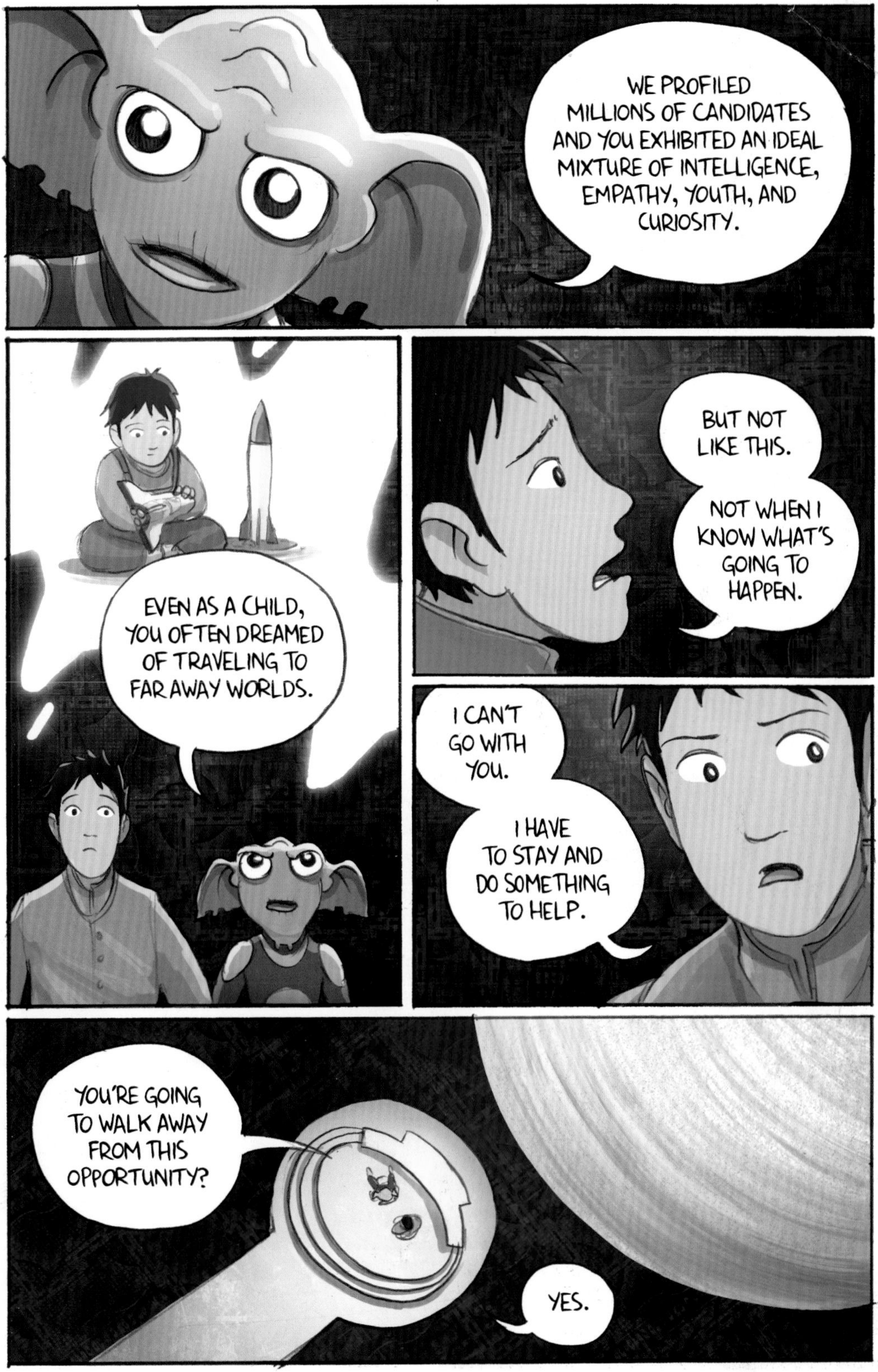
WE PROFILED MILLIONS OF CANDIDATES AND YOU EXHIBITED AN IDEAL MIXTURE OF INTELLIGENCE, EMPATHY, YOUTH, AND CURIOSITY.
EVEN AS A CHILD, YOU OFTEN DREAMED OF TRAVELING TO FAR AWAY WORLDS.
BUT NOT LIKE THIS.
NOT WHEN I KNOW WHAT'S GOING TO HAPPEN.
I CAN'T GO WITH YOU.
I HAVE TO STAY AND DO SOMETHING TO HELP.
YOU'RE GOING TO WALK AWAY FROM THIS OPPORTUNITY?
YES.

GOOD.

GOOD? YOU'RE NOT UPSET?

IT'S YOUR CHOICE, MY FRIEND.

MY JOB IS TO TRAVEL ACROSS THE UNIVERSE AND PRESERVE LIFE.

TAP TAP

AND THERE'S MORE THAN ONE WAY TO ACCOMPLISH THAT.

GOOD LUCK, JAMES.

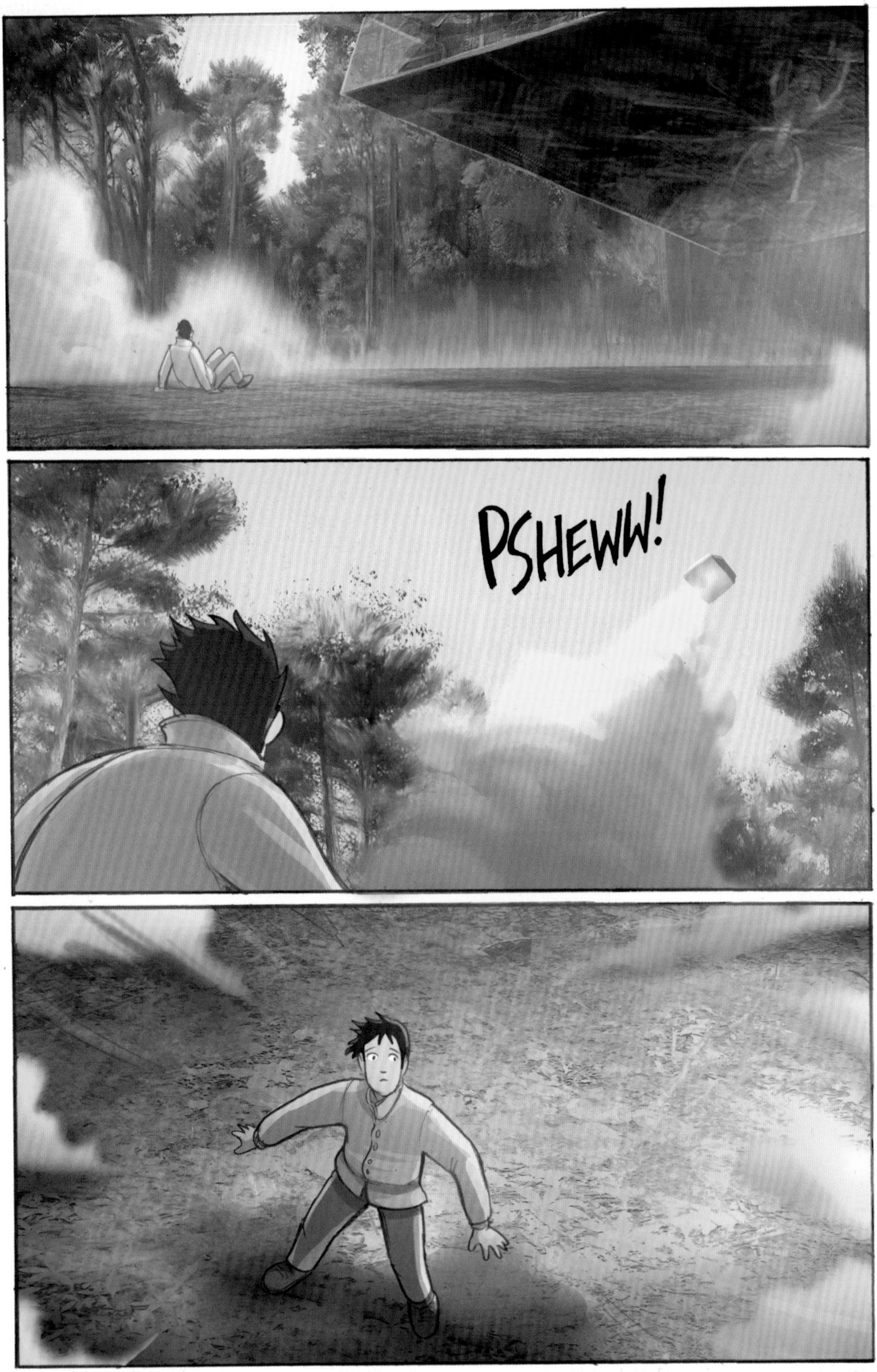
PSHEWW!

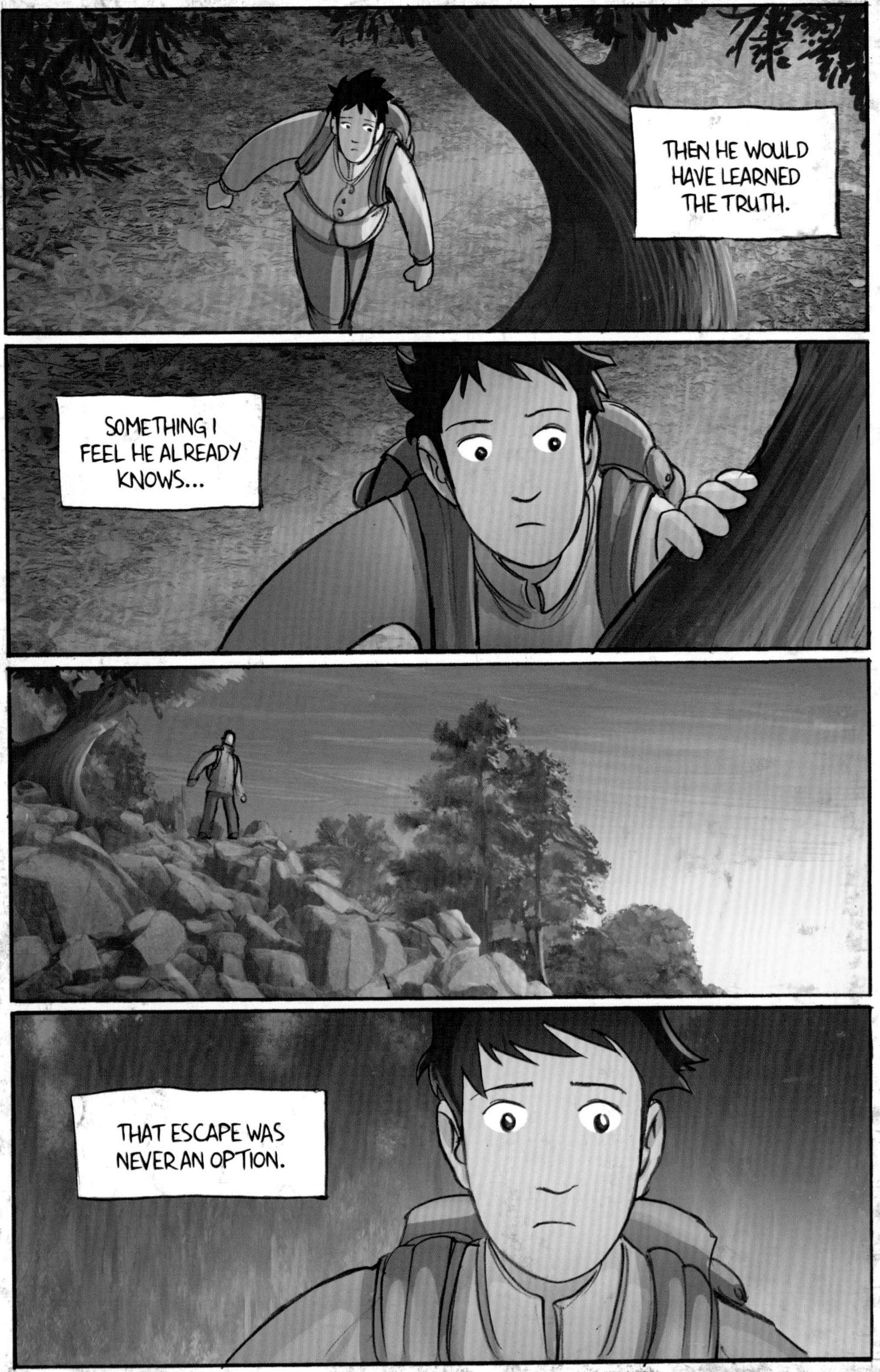
THEN HE WOULD HAVE LEARNED THE TRUTH.
SOMETHING I FEEL HE ALREADY KNOWS...
THAT ESCAPE WAS NEVER AN OPTION.

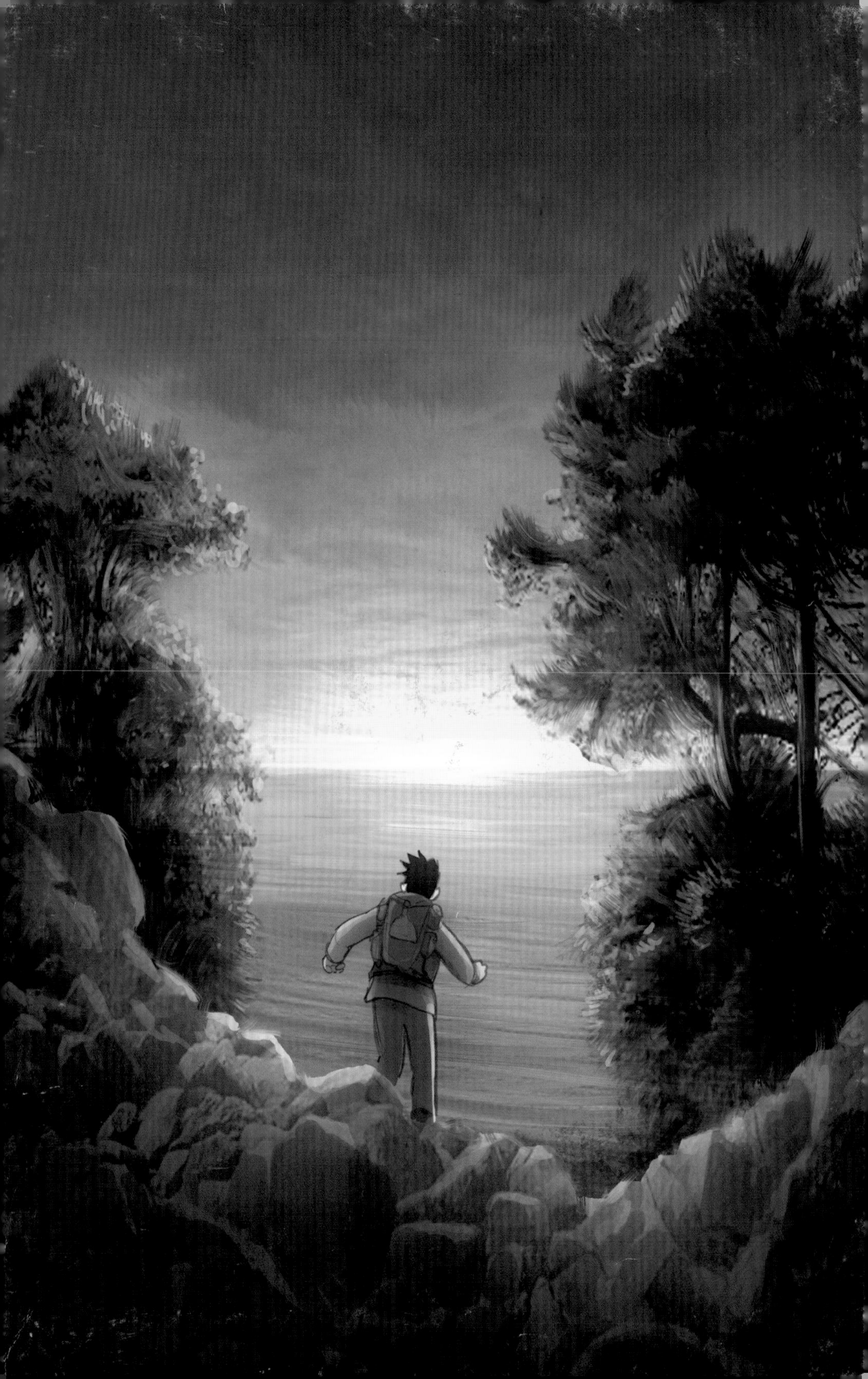

ABOUT THE CREATORS

JASON CAFFOE is a graduate of the Savannah College of Art and Design and a contributor to the *Flight* anthologies. He works as the lead production assistant for Kazu Kibuishi, contributing colors and background art to the *Amulet* series. He also worked on Jake Parker's middle-school graphic novel *Missile Mouse*. Visit him at www.jasoncaffoe.com.

EMILY CARROLL is an up-and-coming artist who works in animation for children's television. She is a contributor to *The Anthology Project*, vol. 2, and her comics and art can also be found at www.emcarroll.com.

KAZU KIBUISHI is the creator of *Amulet*, the award-winning *New York Times*–bestselling middle-school graphic novel series. He was also the editor and art director of eight volumes of *Flight*, the groundbreaking, Eisner-nominated graphic anthology. His graphic collection *Copper* is a Junior Library Guild selection, and his earlier work *Daisy Kutter* was named a YALSA Best Book for Young Adults. For more on Kazu, check out www.boltcity.com.

STUART LIVINGSTON is an American Samoan comics and storyboard artist who lives in Los Angeles. He has contributed to both the *Flight* and *Popgun* anthologies and has produced storyboards for Disney, Warner Bros., Cartoon Network, and others. As a lifelong fan of Japanese RPGs, he was most heavily influenced by games like *Final Fantasy VI* and *Chrono Trigger* while making this comic. Visit him at www.stuartlivingston.com.

JOHANE MATTE has worked as a storyboard artist at Nickelodeon and is now at Dreamworks. Her film and television credits include *How to Train Your Dragon* and *Avatar: The Last Airbender*. Her comics work has appeared in several volumes of *Flight*.

DAVE ROMAN is the creator of *Astronaut Academy: Zero Gravity*. He is the coauthor of *The Last Airbender: Zuko's Story* and *X-Men: Misfits* (a *New York Times* bestseller) and also the creator of the teen horror graphic novel *Agnes Quill: An Anthology of Mystery*. Roman is a Harvey Award nominee and an Ignatz Award and Web Cartoonists' Choice Award winner. See more of his work at yaytime.com.

RAD SECHRIST is a cartoonist, a contributor to *Flight*, and a storyboard artist a Dreamworks, where he worked on *Kung Fu Panda II* and *Megamind*.

RAINA TELGEMEIER is the creator of the popular middle-school graphic novel *Smile* which won a 2011 Eisner Award, a 2010 Boston Globe–Horn Book Award Honor, and Children's Choice Book Award. She previously adapted and illustrated *The Baby-Sitters Club* into series of graphic novels. Telgemeier's work has made the YALSA Great Graphic Novels for Teens ALA Top 10 Graphic Novels for Youth, *Kirkus* Best Books, and ALA Notable Children's Book lists. See more of her work at goraina.com.

* * *

SAYMONE PHANEKHAM helped color "Whatzit." He lives in Montreal, Quebec.

STEPHANIE RAMIREZ helped write and color "The Soldier's Daughter." She lives in Los Angeles, where she works as an illustrator and character designer in animation.